The Black Rose Returns

A murderer stalks the seaside town of Palmetto Bay

BOOK THREE

AGNES MAKÓCZY

For information contact :
www.agnes-makoczy.com

Book Cover Image by George Hodan who has released this "Old Boat In Storm" image under Public Domain license.

https://www.publicdomainpictures.net/en/view-image.php?image=172406&picture=old-boat-in-storm

Book formatting by Derek Murphy from www.CreativIndie.com

ISBN: 0977439585
First Edition: August 2016

Contents

Introduction

The Storm

MARK DRISKOLL COULDN'T SLEEP. Something was different. Something had changed. Perhaps the waves were rougher, or the wind whistled a little louder. He turned sideways on his uncomfortable cabin bunk and tried to settle down. The air had cooled down considerably, and he reached for his quilt and pulled it over his shoulder hoping that now he would be able to drift off. But he couldn't get the images of the beheadings out of his mind. There had been so much blood. Sleep just wouldn't come. Of course it didn't help that the sloop was groaning as if it was about to fall apart.

So he gave up with frustration and got up from his bunk. The movements of the waves were getting more and more erratic. He hung on to a low beam to keep from falling, and a worried look crossed his young, handsome face. There was something wrong with the way the ship moved. Something was definitely off.

Dinner was not sloshing around in his stomach because he had already thrown that up overboard earlier, right after the massacre, but the violent movements of the ship nauseated him, and he desired to heave anyway.

Avoiding the books falling from the shelves, and the other random objects being tossed around the cabin like nature's playthings, Mark Driskoll reached for the one remaining thing on the desk: his brown leather-bound diary. You had to be a fool not to know what was going on out there and what your odds of surviving it were. But taking things in stride, as any brave Englishman would, he grabbed his waist pouch and strapped it on. Wrapping his diary in the best oilskin he could find in a hurry, he slipped that between his chest and his shirt and hoped it would stay safe and dry. That—and the few gold pieces in his purse—would be all he needed in an emergency. Careful not to bang his head on the low beams, he opened the door of his cabin and went outside.

To say that a storm was raging would have been a waste of words. Rather, it looked like he had stepped into a madness in which the world had become a cesspool of angry gray water and the sloop was its toy thing.

With a superhuman effort, he made it up the last few steps that separated his small cabin from the deck. The waves pounded the ship, and the winds tried to blow him back down to his cabin, but he hung on, determined to get up on deck and see for himself what was going on.

The sky was almost completely dark in spite of the time of the day. He tasted the rough salt in between his teeth as he swallowed mouthfuls of the seawater slapping his face. Waves swept through the slippery deck methodically, but still he held on. Staring at the thunderclouds and the lightning that spilled from them, he counted the seconds between the strikes and realized that the worst of the storm was barely a few minutes away. But truly there was nowhere to go. There was no use pretending that he could save himself. Might as well man up and meet his Maker bravely and quit shivering like a schoolgirl.

But it was the aloneness that hit him the deepest. It grabbed at his chest—strangling his soul—and he had to push down the sudden panic rising from it. He was all alone on the sloop. The deck was completely deserted. His first thought was that the drunken sailors, caught by surprise, had been swept overboard. Then he considered the two little boats, stolen earlier from the merchant ship, and strapped precariously somewhere out back to the rigging. He figured that they could have launched those and left him to drown if they had noticed the storm approaching with enough time.

Mark Driskoll stood in the doorway undecided, trying to think. The growling sounds of the storm were deafening, but above those, a noise coming from the cargo hold a few feet away caught his attention. He thought he heard people screaming, and he paid attention. Then he remembered that the slaves had been locked in and—like him—they had probably been forgotten, or simply left behind to die.

There was nothing he could do about it. The wind was too strong, and he would never make it to the padlocked cargo hold without being swept away by the angry waves. But he reconsidered. He was as good as dead already. No harm in trying. He screamed back *I'm coming* but his words were swallowed by the wind. On all fours, and hanging on to whatever he could find, he reached the padlock, but it was tight, and it refused to open. The sheets of rain kept slapping his face, and the saltwater burned in his throat and his eyes, blinding him. But he refused to give up.

The slaves were desperate. He could hear their cries and their prayers above the howling wind. There were children down there too. They banged on the trap door, begging to be let out. Mark didn't even dare think of the terror they were going through in the total darkness below, feeling that the storm was raging on, but knowing that they were trapped and would be unable to get out. Eventually, the sloop would turn on its side, and it would begin to sink. The cargo hold would begin to fill with water and soon the slaves' ankles would be sloshing in it.

Then, faster and faster, the level of the water would rise—filling the cargo hold with the freezing, cold water—and it would reach their knees and then their waists. And they would know there was no place to escape to, and they would huddle against the fear of the rising water, and they would pray, the women holding the terrified children against their breasts. Prayers would give them a little hope, for a little while at least, because you never did lose that last glimmer of hope, and they would pray and chant their hymns and their native songs, and the water would continue rising, relentlessly. By then only a tiny corner of the sloop would have a bubble of air left, and the strong would push the weak away to get to the barely breathable air, not caring that they were condemning them to drown.

Then, more and more of the weak, probably the women and the children, would be pushed away to certain death, and the live ones would be fewer and fewer. But eventually all the air would be gone, and there would be nowhere to go as the sloop slipped faster and faster to the bottom of the sea. The next morning, after the storm was gone, looking at the bright blue sky and the calm, gentle sea, nobody would suspect that three dozen slaves and one lonely Englishman had drowned—abandoned—in fear and agony on a broken ship. All traces of them would have vanished. Mark swallowed hard and shook the terror off. He had to try to get them out of there, no matter what.

He looked up at the sky. The worst of the storm was approaching. Now, one lightning strike followed the next with just seconds in between. Struggling pointlessly against time, he wiggled the padlock with one hand while he held on to a protruding piece of wood. It wasn't working, but—obsessed now—he couldn't let it go. He felt he ought to keep trying. He kept looking around for something to beat the padlock with, and suddenly, he spotted a long, thin piece of metal stuck in the nets.

There was nothing to do but to go fetch the metal bar. The wind was brutal. Fighting the waves of water and the cutting spray in his nose and his eyes, he managed to crawl to the piece of metal and retrieve it. Then, knowing how easily he would be swallowed by the sea if he didn't hold on to something, he tangled himself in the rigging so he could work with both hands.

He beat and beat the padlock, fighting the fury of the storm, slipping and falling, and then slipping again. His mind already knew what his heart wouldn't accept, that the poor devils were going to go down with the broken sloop and stay at the bottom of the sea for all eternity.

He was getting dizzy with the exhaustion and the violent tossing of the sea. He couldn't continue, and he stopped. He dropped the metal bar, and it fell with a reverberating clang. His hands were bleeding, and yet he had accomplished nothing. The slaves screamed on and prayed. But he, Mark Driskoll, was done living. He looked up at the mast and the canvas torn to shreds and admired its dreary beauty against the pinkish, purplish light of the hidden moon. It was over.

Then, he saw the little monkey screeching with terror up the top of the mainmast, dressed in its carnival best, somehow still wearing its little red fez hat. He'd forgotten all about little Maddock. Poor little monkey. It might survive for a while as it was tossed about the seas, as lightweight as a little monkey can be, especially if it found some flotsam to cling to. But wasn't floating for days and dying from thirst and madness a worse fate than a quick drowning?

Mark Driskoll looked up sadly into the howling darkness and thought about everything he had hoped to accomplish and now never would. At that moment, he heard the infernal crack of the breaking mast that signaled the death of the sloop and knew it was all over. It was all over for him and for little Maddock, and it was all over for every single unfortunate soul below deck. And right he was because at that moment, he saw rise from behind the sloop an impossibly enormous wave that seemed to reach as high as the sky. It came frothing furiously against him and the damaged sloop, and he barely had time to utter a quick prayer before everything went black, and he sank into oblivion.

When Mark opened his eyes, he was floating immobile on his back. The water was cold. The dark blue sky was bright with millions of tiny, shiny stars winking at him. How long had he been floating? He wished he could untangle himself to take a look at the coastline. He was sure he was drifting toward land. There had to be a village out there or something. He could hear snippets of music and civilization floating out into the open waters. But he couldn't move, doomed to drift wherever the flotsam and the currents carried him. Maybe when daylight came, someone would see him and come to save him. He couldn't hear the little monkey crying anymore, and he wondered if it was sleeping or if it was dead.

Mark closed his eyes, lulled by the warmth of the warmer water and the gentle breeze that swept around his face, playing with his eyelashes and his wet hair. That was all he could feel now: his face and his head.

No legs, no arms, no body, as if they were all gone. At least he couldn't feel the fish nibbling on his broken arm anymore. How it had hurt at first. Every bite they took was like a knife cutting off a piece of his flesh. But it didn't hurt anymore. So he closed his eyes and dreamed.

There was the big house on the hill, again. He was back in the same dream: faded green, white trim, gabled roof. There should be a big, black and white hairy dog sleeping on the front porch on the tiny Welcome mat, but it wasn't there. Mark looked around and wondered in his sleep where it had gone.

The old swing was swinging, but there was nobody sitting in it. It must be the wind rocking it. He could hear the tinny, metallic screech of the hinges as they rocked back and forth, back and forth.

The dead tree to the left of the house loomed over the house, the knoll, and the horizon, like an old giant who has seen too much, lived too much, and had gotten tired of it all and died. Its gnarled, twisted branches shivered naked in the breeze even though the sun was shining.

Mark walked around the knoll, knowing in his dream that he had been there before. Half a dozen tombstones behind the house were sinking into the soil. Old fashioned tombstones, so faded you couldn't read the inscriptions. It disturbed him not to be able to read them, and he got closer. He got down on one knee in front of one of them and cleaned the face of the stone with his gloved hand. *Mark*. He could read the name, *Mark*. He continued cleaning. He jumped back and gasped, understanding who the tomb was for. Then, suddenly, the dream changed.

People were arriving. Silent and gloomy, looking down at their feet as they followed the path in front of them, they walked up the knoll with a steady rhythm. They all looked so dreary, dressed in black. Top hats kept the faces of the men in the dark. Women and girls in black crinoline petticoats, too tight to breathe in, climbed the path awkwardly avoiding puddles and clumps of grass. Horses and carriages sat at the bottom of the knoll, waiting listlessly, decked in black cloth, while dozens of blackbirds, perched on the gnarled dead tree overlooking the house, stared at Mark with malevolent eyes. Never veering from the path and never lifting their heads or looking at each other, the mourners silently continued their sinister climb to the top of the knoll. Somewhere in the distance, church bells rang.

Mark followed the mourners into the house. It was an open coffin viewing. He stood in line behind them. Nobody said a word. Nobody made a comment. They stepped up to the coffin, looked at the dead man, and then stepped away. When Mark got to the coffin, he looked down at the dead man and wondered why he looked so familiar. The body was mangled under the Sunday suit, the blood seeping out through the seams. The head was bruised, barely human anymore. But those eyes! The dead man stared back at him with his dull, milky eyes that looked so familiar.

Then the pallbearers came to get the coffin and carried it to the back of the house. Mark followed the men to where a big rectangular pit had been dug at the foot of the tombstone inscribed with his name. *Mark, Mark. Who is this Mark?* He wondered. They lowered the coffin into the raw soil and Mark started to scream. *Wait! Screw the lid on. You forgot to put the lid on.* But nobody looked at him, as if he wasn't even there.

He approached the open grave and looked down at the familiar man staring up at him with his dead eyes. *Tell them to stop*, the dead man begged. *Don't let them bury me. Tell them I'm still here.* And Mark screamed and screamed as the gravediggers shoveled the wet, black soil into the grave and right onto the dead man's face.

Mark woke up crying and looked up at the morning sky tinged with the soft pinks and yellows of the upcoming dawn through salt-and-tear-crusted eyelids. Another never-ending day and no hope of death. He closed his aching eyes against the bright morning sun and held the shivering little monkey Maddock—surprised that it had somehow managed to swim to him—and they floated on, always a little closer to land, but always too far to be seen. He tried to comfort the monkey, but his tongue was too swollen to talk. Maybe they would both be lucky today, and they would either be rescued or they would die.

Day One

Flash Flood Warning

MARGO FONTAINE STOPPED SINGING and turned the music off. It just dawned on her that it had been miles and miles since she had driven by the last gas station, and now she looked at the fuel gauge and the blinking warning light with dismay. She was running out of gas. How could she have let this happen? She was daydreaming with Jack again, that was how. It was this lonely stretch of Louisiana highway that reminded her so much of the many times she had driven back to Half Moon Bay, hoping that she would see him again. She had allowed herself to be carried away by her memories.

But no wishful thinking would ever bring Jack back. It had been first a youthful fantasy, and then a wish almost fulfilled. But now Jack was gone forever, probably dead out there somewhere in the war-torn desert, and here she was, driving toward Pierre in hopes of turning a new leaf in her life, in search of that ever-elusive happiness.

A shiver of dread ran through her body, and she turned her attention to the red warning light. She wondered what she was going to do. As far as she could remember, there hadn't been another car on this lonely stretch of road for at least a half hour.

She could always call Brooks for help, but she had no idea where she was. What would she tell him? All she could see was a narrow, endless road without a name, and very bad weather coming. Already the clouds gathering on ahead were getting darker and uglier by the minute, threatening a violent downpour, and the wind was picking up. She could feel the gusts as they hit the car. At least she knew for sure there was no hurricane coming. It looked like the usual Louisiana thunderstorm. But what if she really ran out of gas? What if the storm hit before she could get to safety? What if a flash flood came out of nowhere and swept her car away, and unable to escape, she drowned? Was death by drowning painful? Was it quick? She tightened her hands on the wheel and tried not to panic.

She was driving straight into the storm, and there was nothing she could do about it. Looking at the ugly black clouds ahead, she quickly considered her options and realized that turning back was not one of them. She didn't have enough gas for that. Besides, the road was too narrow to turn the big Mercedes around, and the ditches on the side were too deep. She would probably slip off the road and then what? Wait to die of drowning in the gutter? Her only option was to keep on going and find a safe place to stop.

Up ahead, the sun had just about vanished, filling the sky with a threatening gloom. She grabbed the wheel tighter, struggling against the wind that pushed the car sideways toward the ditch. Pouring out of the angry clouds, lightning brightened the sky and shook the car violently. She had to get off the road. But where? There was not an inhabited town, not a gas station, not a turn-off. But she had to do something. She pushed down her increasing anxiety and kept on driving.

She was in the middle of nowhere. But then, when you drive the Louisiana back roads, you often are in the middle of nowhere. All she had seen for miles and miles were abandoned farmlands that time had turned to shrub. Scattered around the landscape, you could see—here and there—a rotting barn or a horse shed, leaning away from the wind, deteriorating under the wild Louisiana weather, unfit for shelter. If there had ever been farming communities around, they were all gone now.

A big fat raindrop plopped on her windshield, and then another one. The rain had arrived. She fumbled with the unfamiliar controls trying to remember Brooks' instructions about turning the windshield wipers on. Drat. This is what happens when your chauffeur insists on driving you everywhere. She was a stranger in her own car.

At the end of yet another abandoned little town, she stopped under a decaying railway bridge and fiddled with the controls until she got the windshield wipers and the headlights working. It was amazing how dark the sky had gotten in just a few minutes. And more bad luck. The GPS was on a search-can't-locate loop and refused to work.

Should she stay under the crumbling bridge until the storm passed? It seemed more of a hazard than a safe location. But surely, if there was a railroad bridge, there was a town nearby. Wasn't that the way it worked? She kept on driving tentatively for a couple of miles, looking to her right and her left, scrutinizing the road for a road sign, a turn-off, or a mile marker. Sometimes, turn-offs meandered parallel to the railway tracks for a while and eventually led somewhere.

She was so distracted by her musings that she almost missed it. Suddenly, behind some overgrown shrub, a narrow road, its entrance almost covered by weeds appeared out of the monotonous landscape, and without overthinking it, she turned the wheel.

She swerved sharply to the right. But the movement was too sudden, and the back of the big, heavy Mercedes skidded on the moist, sandy blacktop. She held the wheel tightly in her sweaty palms and rejected the urge to slam on the brakes. Her heart hammered in her chest as the car swerved first to one side and then the other. Still, she held on tight.

By now, a steady rain began drumming on the car's rooftop, and the wind whirled up twigs and dry leaves that banged on her windshield, getting entangled in the wipers. Margo's hands shook as she struggled with the skidding tires and the diminishing visibility.

Time stopped briefly as it seemed that Margo was going to careen off the road, slipping, sliding, getting ever closer to the edge. But by a last-minute reprieve, she managed to straighten the car and sang out a grateful *Hallelujah!* She had been this close to ending up in that ditch. Now, if only her gas would last long enough to get there—somewhere—all would be well.

The back road she was following was surrounded on both sides with tall forest trees whose tops got lost in the rainy haze. Their fronds swayed and shook with the wind and threatened to snap off and throw themselves at her car. The wind howled and shrieked, and her heartbeats pounded in her brain as she held on tight. But a sudden burst of sunlight shone at the end of the road and she realized that she was almost there, wherever there was. She could already see the angry, frothy sea at the bottom of the sloping decline. She wasn't that far at all. She would be there in a few minutes. She exhaled the breath she had been holding in forever. She was going to be safe.

The momentary relief was very short, though. The brunt of the storm came down much faster than Margo expected. It went from a few steady drops to a vicious downpour in a matter of seconds, and the sun vanished completely. The windshield wipers beat the water away in a patterned staccato but they were not fast enough. Soon, she could barely see a foot ahead of her. A river of water, running down the slope with her, threatened to wash the car away. The winds kept getting stronger. They howled over the rhythmic thump-thump of the windshield wipers.

Margo slowed down to crawling mode and drove in the middle of the road with shaking hands gripping the wheel. She barely dared to breathe. She wiped one sweaty hand on her pants and then the other. Her knuckles were white, and her eyes hurt from all the squinting. The minutes seemed to last forever, and on and on she drove, focused on remaining in the middle of the road, keeping the car steady so it wouldn't get washed away.

She finally reached the end of the road at the bottom of the incline and paused at a small circular roundabout that appeared out of the pouring rain as if it had been a phantom materializing out of the fog. In front of her, and in the center of the roundabout, stood a nondescript stone or concrete statue barely visible in the all-encompassing rain, and beyond that—presumably—the slate-gray sea.

Catching a big lungful of air, Margo rested her head gratefully on the headrest and waited for her heart to calm down. Her whole body was shaking, especially her hands. She could feel every heartbeat pounding in her temples. She was in overdrive.

To her left, an almost empty parking lot in front of a beat down hotel seemed inviting enough, and she parked as close to the front door as she could. Suddenly, she was so relieved that she had decided to leave her cats Ice and Fenway at home, even though they liked Pierre and would have enjoyed spending a few days with him in his Cypremort Point bungalow. At least they were home and safe. She picked up her cell phone and dialed.

"Lucy, it's Margo," she told her housekeeper, screaming over the roar of the storm. "I got caught in the rain and had to stop, but I'm okay."

"So where are you now?"

"I have no idea yet. I took the only turn-off I could find and now I'm in front of an old hotel in some little town by the beach. I'll stay here until the storm passes."

"Mr. Pierre just called. He was worried about you driving in the bad weather."

"Lucy, can you hear me? Oh, there you are. The reception's really bad."

"Yes. I can barely hear you. It's raining cats and dogs here as well. I said Mr. Pierre just called."

"I heard you." Margo turned the windshield wipers off. "There. That's better," she said. "Please call him and tell him I have to reschedule. Hello? Lucy?"

Margo stared at her phone in anger. She played with the buttons and she shook it, but nothing. The line had gone dead. Well, at least she had managed to tell Lucy that she was safe, and Lucy could let Pierre know as well.

She sat still for a bit and watched the rain come down. It was a wall of water. It felt like the whole world was going to wash away. She could sit in the car and wait the storm out. But as much as she dreaded getting out and facing the gale, there was no way to know how long the rain would last. She would be better off indoors where there was a chance to eat something and use the restroom. She steeled herself. Grabbing purse, keys, and phone, and with shoes in hand, she jumped out of the car and faced the storm.

The coldness of the rain and the strength of the wind caught her by surprise. The drops felt like ice needles as they lashed her body and scraped her skin. Clutching her purse and her shoes, she put her head down to better push against the wind. She was running in three, four inches of water that swirled around her ankles for a few seconds and then headed furiously downhill toward the ocean, threatening to pull her along. Pebbles dug into the soles of her naked feet, and she banged her toes on the cement curb when she reached it, but she got to the door. She was soaking wet to the bone, but she was okay.

The Drunken Duck Pub and Hotel, she read out loud through the falling curtain of water, eyeing the peeling gold colors painted on a wildly swinging sign in front of the door. It portrayed what looked like a drunken duck holding a frothy jug of beer. She pushed the heavy glass door and entered. A raft of wet wind and dry leaves spilled into the room with her and then slammed the door shut behind her.

The Drunken Duck Pub

ABOUT A DOZEN UNSHAVED FACES stared up blankly at her, surprised at the unexpected intrusion. They were scattered about the establishment in groups of two or three around round tables and wooden chairs, nursing beer mugs and small bowls of peanuts. Empty peanut shells lay discarded carelessly on the chipped black and white checkerboard tiles under them. The mild odor of unwashed bodies mingled with that of stale booze and the cloying tang of mildew, always present in older wooden houses in the South.

Large windows on two expansive walls, beaten by the sheets of rain coming at them, gave the place a gloomy, unfriendly atmosphere in spite of all the lights that were on, and in spite of the toe-tapping chanky-chank of the Cajun music spewing from the old fashioned jukebox in the corner. Low tree branches appeared intermittently from the rising fog and slapped at the windows, scratching the glass-like monsters trying to come in. Margo shivered.

"Hello everyone," she told the unenthusiastic crowd, and she raised a hand and waved.

"What on earth are you doing here, *étrangère*, in this weather?" the bartender asked.

"*La bebelle est perdue*," someone said and everyone laughed. Margo scrunched her eyebrows. How was that funny?

"How can she be lost when this is the only road to nowhere?" People laughed again.

"I was heading for Cypremort Point," she told them with a hopeless shrug. She wiped wet hair out of her face and looked down self-consciously at the puddle of dirty water under her bare feet. "But I was running out of gas, and then the storm came, and I hoped there would be a hotel or a restaurant somewhere to wait it out. And a gas station," she added. Everyone laughed again. Margo looked at them baffled.

"Don't pay any attention to them, sha," the bartender told her with a friendly grin. She was a plump, pretty, middle-aged woman with her hair up in a disheveled bun. "They've had too many beers. There's no gas station in Palmetto Bay, but someone ought to have enough gas in their backyard tanks to help out a stranger."

"Am I very far from Cypremort Point?" she asked the bartender.

"You could be on the other side of the world at this moment, for all the good it would do you. The little bridge isn't safe in this weather and might not be for days. Unless you want to go all the way back up to the highway and go from there. But that's not safe either. Can I offer you something to drink?"

"I'd love some coffee. It was a rough drive."

"I was about to have some *café au lait* myself. Come sit with me, and we can talk while I work. But first, I'm going to get you something dry to wear." While Josie the bartender fetched her some dry clothes, Margo looked around the establishment. People stopped staring at her and quickly looked into their glasses, pretending to be minding their own business. But way at the back, close to the jukebox, two men continued staring at her. One of them was enormous and unfriendly looking. The other one looked angry.

At that moment, Josie stepped back into the room and handed her the clothes. She followed Margo's line of sight and said, "That's my husband Billy back there. And the other one is his friend Pete."

"He seems big."

"*Oui, oui.* He's big, and he's very dangerous." Josie was not smiling.

Once she had changed into the dry jeans and t-shirt so kindly offered, Margo followed the woman's invitation to the long, well-polished bar and sat down on a stool and propped her elbows up. A multicolored cat that had been sleeping at the end of the shiny bar top approached her cautiously and sniffed her hands. She rubbed it absentmindedly enjoying the soft, clean, silky fur under her touch.

She was famished. A blackboard leaning against the shiny mirror behind the beer tap fountains advertised in white chalk some homemade boudin and crawfish boules. Her mouth salivated. She watched the coffee pot trickle and brew and inhaled the enticing aroma. The room had gone silent. She knew—without turning around—that everyone was watching her.

"My name is Margo Fontaine," she told the bartender.

"Nice to meet you, Margo Fontaine. My name is Josie Barras. And the sweet kitty you're petting is Pepper Paws. Fontaine isn't a common last name around here. Any relation to Francesc Fontayn?"

"Yes, actually, he was my ancestor. He was quite the adventurer."

"Is he the Fontayn who explored the Caribbean Islands searching for the Fountain of Youth? And then he discovered some indigenous tribes in Mississippi and hidden pyramids in the mosquito-infested jungles of Florida?"

"Yes. That's him. He was the original Indiana Jones. Then he published his memoirs and settled down in Half Moon Bay. That's where I'm from. How did you know?"

"I loved history in high school. Is it true that he found the *Maria Gracia*? And that it was carrying a fortune in gold?"

"That's what they say. The house he built with that gold still stands. The lands are gone, but the house sits right on the water. It's old and decrepit now, but I'm slowly having it restored."

"I love old houses. This hotel is very old too. My great, great, great-grandpa was a slave trader before he reformed and retired, and we've lived in Palmetto Bay since then."

"What's a reformed slave trader?"

"Well, there used to be many plantations around here. Even with the high mortality rate, slave trading was a very lucrative business venture. But one day, right after the birth of his first son, great-grandpa saw a mother separated from her baby at the slave market. It was a turning point in his life. He suddenly realized the cruelty of what he was doing and lost his taste for it."

"That's quite a story."

"*C'est vrai.* So with all his ill-gotten gains, he built this huge house. And the family has lived here ever since, and when times got bad, they converted it into a hotel. Except that now it's crumbling, and there's no one left to repair it. I don't have any children, and my husband Billy's getting old and has no interest in keeping it up."

"Can't you sell it?"

"Oh, no. Who would want to buy it? Nobody comes this way anymore, except for the people who get lost as you did. Ever since Cypremort Point became a popular vacation spot and people started building their weekend camps there, everyone's lost interest in Palmetto Bay."

"That's sad. Does it have a pretty beach, the bay?"

"It does indeed. A few years back, we used to get a lot of tourists. The sand is very fine and white, and the waters are deep blue and translucent. You can see your toes clearly until you are waist-deep. And the water temps are perfect for swimming all the way 'till winter. We've been very lucky that none of the oil slicks have affected us.

"There's a cove nearby that's flooded most of the year, now that the Louisiana coast is sinking, but they say pirates used to keep their treasures there on account of how unreachable it is. Historians say there are hundreds of shipwrecks off of the Shark Bayou coastline."

"And you can't turn that into a tourist attraction?"

"We've tried. I guess our little town is doomed to die. *Quel domage,* too. Because once the sun comes out, you'll see it's like an outpost of paradise."

The phone rang back there somewhere and Josie excused herself. Everyone had remained silent while they talked, eavesdropping for sure. But now, conversations resumed as if they had never ceased. Pepper Paws, installed in Margo's lap like she belonged there, was purring up a storm. She complained every time Margo tried to stop petting her.

She looked around curiously. The old pub was a trip to the past. Dainty antique-looking bottles mingled with the more sleek modern bottles of alcohol on the glass shelves, reflected in the well-polished mirror behind them. The round tables and the bar stools had been glossed to shiny perfection by generations of pants, shirts, and skirts, and the large windows gave an ample view of the furious storm that was battering the bay outside. The jukebox had gone silent.

Margo shivered. Now that she had calmed down, a wave of exhaustion hit her and made her yawn. The people in the pub were still staring at her. They didn't seem to be the friendliest people in the world. Disappointed at being stuck in Palmetto Bay, she thought about her excursion to visit Pierre. It was her first attempt at dating since Jack's disappearance, and look at how it had turned out. She sipped on her coffee and wondered what was taking Josie so long. She was definitely going to have to taste the homemade boudin. Pepper Paws continued to purr happily in her lap.

The Storm

THE BRUNT OF THE STORM ARRIVED about an hour later. Tree limbs and gusts of wind beat at the windows furiously and made them shake. The storm was so loud that it overpowered the hush-hush conversations of the customers and the sound of music from the jukebox that someone had gotten going again. Lights flickered, and everyone in the pub groaned. A big circular yellow sign by the bathrooms that advertised fresh oysters blinked a few times, popped, and then died.

The worst thing ever would be for the electricity to go out. It usually meant that a tree or a branch had fallen on a main electrical power line, and it would take days for the lines to be repaired and the roads to be cleared. Ugh. Margo couldn't cope with the idea of being stuck in this town for so long, so she elevated a quick prayer to Saint Scholastica—the Patron Saint of storms—and decided that it was time to get a room and get some rest. It had been a very long day.

She climbed the stairs to her room followed by her new friend Pepper Paws, who for some strange reason had acquired a shine to her. Carrying the borrowed robe and slippers that Josie—in her kindness—insisted on putting in her hands, she almost crawled upstairs, she was so exhausted.

The converted hotel had once been a mansion of magnificent grandeur. The wallpaper in the stairwell had yellowed with age and was peeling in the occasional spot, but the richness of the chinoiserie pattern on the walls had survived the centuries and lent the circular staircase a dignity and beauty that reminded Margo of her own old Half Moon Bay home.

Very little of the storm could be felt in the stairwell, but as soon as she opened the door to her room, a succession of lightning strikes shook the window panes and illuminated ferociously the room as if it was about to blow the glass out of its frame. Yes, extreme weather in Louisiana liked to announce itself with fanfare.

Pepper Paws didn't seem to mind the weather, and jumped gracefully up on the bed, where she proceeded to bathe herself. *She knows she's so pretty,* Margo thought with a smile. Before adopting Ice and Fenway at her friend Jenny's death, she had never been allowed to have a pet. Her mom, the famous opera singer—The Sublime Nicola Fontaine—was always traveling around the world, and Margo usually went with her. They never had a real home beyond guest houses and hotel rooms. Therefore, a pet had always been out of the question.

She was mesmerized by the chaos beyond her window. She stood at the window for a while—with the lights off so she could see better—staring outside. Occasionally, lightning would strike the horizon illuminating the churning gray waters of Shark Bayou, tossing and foaming restlessly in the dark. The neon lights from the hotel welcome sign and the yellow street light under her window illuminated meagerly the parking lot, and she thought she could see—barely—her car being pounded by the falling rain. She hoped no fishing boats had gotten caught up in the storm, because, on a night like this one, it would surely be a death sentence.

Finally, Margo walked to the night table and turned the light on. She took Jack's picture out of her purse. The gilding on the frame was tarnished away from so much holding and so many tears, but that only made it more precious. Jack smiled back at her, his impish grin frozen in time forever. His beloved dog Paco looked right at the photographer with his tongue lolling. Margo just knew that he had been wagging his tail when the picture was taken. He was a happy dog. His tail was always wagging. She was going on a date with Pierre, but she was still carrying Jack's photograph around. One day she was going to have to stop that.

She looked at the books she had borrowed from the bookshelf in the hallway, but she was too restless to read. She lifted the telephone handset on the night table for the tenth time, and for the tenth time told herself that it was still dead. In Half Moon Bay, Lucy and Brooks were probably worried about her, and she had no way of letting them know what was going on. Her cats, Ice, and Fenway would have nobody to snuggle with tonight. In Lafayette, Pierre would be wondering why she had canceled their rendezvous. Would he be worried about her? She wondered.

Finally, knowing there was no point in struggling against the inevitable, she told Pepper Paws to scoot over and threw herself on top of the patchwork quilt to read a dog-eared copy of Wilkie Collins' gothic novel *The Moonstone*, the perfect book for a scary, stormy night.

In between chapters, she tried the internet, already knowing that there was none. Frustrated and claustrophobic, she tried to focus on the book, but in the back of her mind there was always that feeling of powerlessness to resolve her situation.

But peace came to her eventually as the exhaustion caught up with her. Words on the page started swimming in front of her eyes, and she turned the table lamp off.

The storm raged on, but it seemed to be passing. It was safe enough to close the eyes and go to sleep. Downstairs, the Cajun music was still blaring over the whirling winds, and the drinkers must have been having a good time because she could hear them laugh raucously from time to time. They were obviously planning to stay and drink through the night. Next to her, snuggling and purring gently, Pepper Paws slept contentedly. Finally, all the wild thoughts galloping through her mind settled down, and Margo went to sleep.

Day Two

Aftermath

MARGO WOKE UP TO THE SUN shining in her face. The storm was gone. She looked toward the window and saw water drops glistening on the glass pane. Pepper Paws sat on the window sill, staring outside, watching something with great interest.

Against all odds, the bed had turned out to be cozy and comfortable. She couldn't believe she had slept through the storm. That's how exhausted she must have been. Her seaside town of Half Moon Bay was very much the same: exposed to violent summer storms that came from the sea with fury, oftentimes lashing out and destroying everything in their wake. But the morning after, the sun was out, the sea was calm and quiet as if nothing had happened.

Tightening Josie's robe around her, she approached the window and looked out. It was a beautiful, sunny day. What she could see of the water was deep blue and shimmering under the morning sun. She could almost smell the fresh, salty morning air. She would hit the road right after breakfast, as soon as someone sold her some gasoline. She would call Pierre from the car and salvage her vacation, and let Lucy know that she was okay. She rubbed the cat's soft fur absentmindedly. She could hardly wait to get on the road.

The beach was full of people milling about. Something was going on down there. You could barely see the color of the sand, there were so many of them. Some were looking out to sea. Children and dogs running unsupervised, the adults mesmerized by whatever was out there. Others had formed a tight group around something that lay on the sand, further down the beach. She couldn't see what it was.

She ran downstairs followed by the cat and almost collided with Josie, who was just opening the front door of the pub.

"What's going on out there? The beach is full of people."

"I don't know," Josie said. "But I'm going to find out. Come with me. Let's go see what's going on."

"But I'm wearing your robe and slippers."

"*N'importe pas.* I'll throw them in the washing machine." And she grabbed Margo's arm impatiently and pulled her along. People were milling, loud, and excited. A small girl detached herself from the group on the beach and ran across the little plaza toward them.

"Aunt Josie, Aunt Josie, hurry up." She hopped up and down with excitement. "There's a lady fainted on the beach. Miss Erma says she came from the ship."

"I'm coming, sha. But I have to go and check on something first." The girl scooped Pepper Paws up in her arms and carried the limp cat with her toward the beach. Pepper Paws looked at Margo with despair but allowed herself to be carried away.

Margo followed Josie to the group of people standing by the pier, looking out to sea. They were talking animatedly and pointing in the direction of a sandbank a few hundred yards from the shore, to her left. A man with scraggly hair and beard and threadbare clothes mumbled something about a pirate's curse as he drank something vile-smelling from a small green bottle. An old woman brandishing a Bible in the air wailed about the End of Days and punishment to all.

Margo looked toward the sandbank, and then she had to rub her eyes and look again. An ancient shipwreck had emerged from the belly of the waters and had been dragged by the storm almost all the way to the shore. It rested on its side—crippled and decaying—stuck on the sandbank. Black broken masts hung dismally at an angle, with remnants of rotting sails dangling from them.

"Good morning, Marie," Josie said. The woman standing next to her was holding a pair of binoculars. "What can you see?"

"The sea gave us back the *Camilla Star*. Imagine, after all these years."

"Are you sure it's the Camilla Star?"

"See for yourself," Marie said and handed Josie the binoculars. Josie looked and shook her head in amazement. "Yes, it is the Camilla Star," she said, sounding surprised. "So Billy was right."

"Amazing what good condition it is in after all this time underwater."

"Yes. It must have been lying in dead water. No oxygen, no rotting, no corrosion."

Josie turned in Margo's general direction and explained.

"Very early this morning, my husband Billy and a couple of other fishermen sighted the ship on the sandbank. They alerted the others and left a while ago to see if there's something they can salvage."

"So that's why they're rowing over there?" Margo approached the two women and asked Josie, "Isn't that dangerous?"

"Yes, it's very dangerous. When my husband Billy and his friends were young, a ship appeared on that same sandbank after a big storm. They all rowed out and explored the ship. One of their friends died, trapped under a log. And they didn't even find much worth salvaging.

"But this ship is different. According to the one lone survivor who wrote in his journal about it, the Camilla Star was a pirate ship in disguise that had just attacked and looted a merchant ship full of gold coins. I told you I read a lot of history." She looked at Margo and grinned. "The men will try to recover the treasure—if it's still on board—before the coast guard and the reporters get here, and who knows who else swoops in and cordons it off."

"What do you mean?"

"That you never know. Once the news gets out, the government will send someone to confiscate whatever we find. They might say they'll look into ownership and all that. The point is that someone will come and take charge, and we'll never see the treasure again. Assuming that it exists, of course.

THE BLACK ROSE RETURNS

"The survivor's journal mentions that the Camilla Star was carrying slaves and whiskey. We can get the barrels of whiskey out if they're still intact. There might be other stuff worth bringing ashore as well. They only have two, three days at the most until someone finds out the Camilla Star has resurfaced, or it slips back into the sea."

"How amazing. Would that whiskey still be good, though?"

"I don't see why not if the barrels survived. The odds of finding them intact are small. But we should know by this afternoon."

"Will the locals keep the secret from leaking?"

"Oh yes. This is our treasure now. Nobody will tell. This town is dying, Margo. They all know how badly we need the money if we want it to survive a little longer."

Josie tore herself away from the sight of the shipwreck. She wasn't smiling anymore. She had a faraway, haunted look in her eyes. Margo could tell that she was worried. Her husband was probably too old to be wading into rotting shipwrecks.

"Let's go see this woman who washed ashore," she told Margo. She pushed and elbowed her way to the front of the crowd on the beach to take a closer look, pulling on Margo's sleeve as she went. There on the sand lay the young blonde woman, the one that old Erma swore had come from the sea. Her eyes were closed as if she were sleeping, her white Edwardian gown soaking wet. Her bare feet were sandy, but blood had seeped through the white sand stuck to them, where she had scratched herself on the pebbles or the flotsam.

"Pepper Paws, get back here," Margo hissed toward the cat who was sniffing the girl's eyelashes. When the cat ignored her, she took a couple of steps toward the cat and bent down to pick her up.

On close-up, the girl was beautiful. Her long honey-colored hair was spread out around her head like a halo, in a tangled mess of sand and seaweed. Salt crystals sparkled on her blond eyebrows and eyelashes. Her nightgown was badly torn. On one shoulder, where the dress had torn away, you could see clearly delineated, the tattoo of a black rose. Self-consciously—feeling like she was intruding—she quickly stood up and stepped back.

"What happened?"

"She walked out of the water," an older woman told her. "I was looking at the shipwreck, and then I saw this woman walk out of the water. She came from the ship."

"That's impossible, Erma. You must be mistaken," Josie told her firmly and shook her head in disbelief. "The Camilla Star went down in the year 1880. This woman must have come from somewhere else." Josie put a hand over her eyes, like a visor, and scrutinized the tranquil sea, looking for a boat or a yacht, or an explanation.

The woman called Erma got angry. "I know what I saw, Josie. I'm not that old. And I'm not blind."

"Okay, Erma, I'm sorry. So tell me what happened."

"Well, I was all alone out here, walking my Alfie and watching the boys row toward the shipwreck when I noticed someone coming out of the water. She gave me a regular scare. I thought it was a ghost.

"I started walking in her direction. She looked ill. Before I got to her, she stumbled on the rocks over there, and she fell, but she got up and kept on walking. She kept stumbling on the hem of her gown that she's wearing. It was soaking wet and she was having a hard time with it." Margo—whose full-length robe had gotten sandy and was soaking wet on the bottom—knew what old Erma was talking about. That heavy cotton nightgown must have been hard to drag and pull soaking wet. It was quite a miracle that it hadn't dragged the girl down in the water and drowned her.

"I called to her, but she didn't answer. I tried to get to her faster, but there is so much debris on the sand." Erma lifted her shoulders helplessly and looked up at Josie. "I watched her walk a few more feet, and then she collapsed."

"Did anyone else see what happened?" Josie asked the onlookers. They all shook their heads. No, no, they said, nobody saw anything. "Besides, nobody walks out of the sea just like that. Erma is getting old and seeing things," Marie said.

Josie stared at the woman on the sand, and everyone watched Josie as if she was the oracle. The collective held their breath and waited for her to speak.

"Extraordinary," she finally said. "I could swear I've seen this woman before."

"Who is she?" someone asked.

"She's the spitting image of Striker Grott's mother. Look at her. Look at the black rose."

The crowd oohed and aahed unbelievingly. They got closer. So did Margo.

"Who is this Mr. Grott?" she asked.

"He's Joseph Striker Grott, but whoever doesn't call him Master Grott, calls him Striker. He's the man who lives in the big house on the hill."

"And this woman looks like his mother?"

"*Mais oui*. She's the spitting image of his mother Maude."

Pepper Paws jumped out of Margo's arms and approached the girl again. One of her hands was carelessly tossed outward, semi-open. The cat seemed fascinated by it and took turns sniffing it and looking at Margo poignantly as if trying to tell her something.

"What it is, Pepper? What do you see?" Margo got down on her knees next to the cat and stuck her face close to the open hand. The fingernails were clean and carefully trimmed. It was a delicate hand, a hand well cared for. Manicured perhaps? This was not a girl who did manual labor.

"What do you see, Pepper?" she asked again. The cat looked at her and meowed impatiently. So Margo bent down again and looked. The nightgown was well sown. The cuff was somewhat frayed, but the stitches seemed handmade. Were there any sewing machines one hundred and fifty years ago? She believed yes, but probably many people still hand-stitched their garments. Many vintage clothing shops sold old fashioned nightgowns, nothing extraordinary there. So what had caught the cat's attention?

She looked at Pepper Paws and realized that everyone had gone silent. They probably thought she was nuts, there down on her knees, talking to a cat. But Pepper kept at it, mewling more and more irritably, insisting, looking into her eyes, trying hard to tell her something, so she stuck her face to the hand again, and this time she saw it. In very faint blue ink there was a faded series of numbers, almost gone now. And she could have sworn it was a telephone number.

"Pepper, you're a genius. We are going to have to have a chat with our castaway when she wakes up."

Meantime, someone had walked over to Josie and asked, "Is she alive?"

Josie approached the young woman, squatted in front of her, and touched her neck with an open hand. "Oh, yes," she said as she got back up. "She is very much alive." A restless murmur ran through the crowd.

The Shipwreck

AFTER THEY CARRIED THE YOUNG WOMAN to the infirmary on a stretcher, the crowd dispersed, and the dogs ran away, and Margo returned to the pub with Josie and Pepper Paws, padding awkwardly in the now wet and sandy slippers. Out there on the sandbank, the fishermen had arrived at the ship, and all the little rowing boats were lined up, some pulled up on the sand, the others tied to each other, and to the rotting ropes of the Camilla Star.

"So Josie, who was this Maude you were talking about?" she asked, plopping herself on one of the stools in front of the bar counter. Josie picked up a rag and started polishing the long, shiny bar with practiced movements. Pepper leaped first onto a bar stool, and from there to the top, where she got herself comfy conveniently close to Margo's hands. She nuzzled them, reminding Margo that Princess Pepper Paws needed to be petted.

"She was the present Mr. Grott's mother. She was said to have been beautiful and lonely. Her husband was always gone on business. So she lived up at the big house with too much time on her hands.

"There's an enormous portrait of her in the main hall of the big house. Striker Grott worships that portrait and has never allowed it to be moved. It sits over the main fireplace which is never lit so the portrait won't be damaged. Not that it would, you know, but he won't allow it.

"But let me tell you. He might have been a self-centered, selfish, spoiled young man who had no respect for anyone. But he did love his mother dearly. Those who knew him when he was young hinted that— more than love—it was an unholy obsession."

"Really!"

"*Mais well*, they say he was heartbroken when she vanished. And there were all kinds of rumors floating around. If her disappearance had happened today, they would have questioned him at the very least, but back then, he was the law of the land, and his family owned the whole parish, so nobody asked him where his mother went, and the beautiful Mrs. Grott was never seen again. The funny thing is that the girl on the beach had the exact same black rose tattooed on the exact same shoulder. Go figure." Josie looked puzzled.

"What about Striker Grott's dad?"

"I have no idea. Now that you mention it, I wonder whatever happened to him. I think I remember some old-timer mentioning that he disappeared about the same time as the beautiful Maude. But I might be mistaken. I have to warn you that in Palmetto Bay rumors and innuendo mingle freely with the truth, and they're not always easy to tell apart.

"Mais well, when the Camilla Star left Louisiana in the late 1870's it was carrying sugar cane from the Grott plantation. Usually, after dropping off the sugar cane, the ships would pick up cargoes of slaves, or silks, or furniture, for him.

"On its last trip back, we know that the Camilla Star stopped on the island of Martinique and picked up some whiskey. They also picked up a couple of passengers, one of whom survived the storm and wrote the journal. This is how we know that soon after leaving Martinique the Captain flew the red Jolly Roger flag and attacked a merchant ship. His sailors killed everyone on board and absconded with the cargo of slaves and several chests of gold coins."

"On the way here though, they got caught in a bad storm. Sea Captains were too daring those days, more than happy to sail during the stormy season regardless of the dangers if the price was right, and they didn't mind putting everyone's lives at risk."

"So the Camilla Star sunk with the slaves and the treasure."

"*Oui, oui*. It was a bad year for New Orleans and Palmetto Bay. The storm devastated the coast and swept away thousands of people, animals, and houses. The Camilla Star never made it back here. We don't know where it went down, except it was somewhere between Martinique and the Louisiana coast.

"Everyone around here lost someone on the Camilla Star. Young men used to flock to New Orleans to sail on those big, fancy boats. They thought it was such a grand adventure, to sail the seven seas, to see the world. The pay was good if you survived, plus you came back like a hero, and girls loved to marry a sailor."

"And that's what was in the journal?"

"*Oui, oui.* That in a nutshell. Old Mr. Grott was rich, powerful, and cruel. His wife had vanished: just another Grott woman to disappear suspiciously off the face of the earth. She ran away some said, was murdered by her husband, said others. Mais well, nobody ever saw her again either. She vanished about the same time that the Camilla Star left New Orleans for the last time. Maybe she wasn't murdered at all and instead left Louisiana on that ship. We'll never know."

Margo sat on her bar stool sipping on her café au lait, rubbing the cat obediently, thinking that it was time to get dressed and get on the road. From where she sat, she had a sweeping view of a clear stretch of the crystalline blue water and the numerous Bonaparte Gulls floating lazily on it.

It was very strange, the story of this young woman appearing on the sand like that. Not that she believed for a second that she had actually walked out of the sea. There was no such thing. But the rose tattoo business was bizarre. What was she playing at?

"Has the stranger regained consciousness?" she asked when Josie brought her own coffee over.

"Not yet. But I'm sure we'll find out as soon as she does. In the meantime, I'm sorry to have to tell you that you're stuck here for a while."

"What do you mean stuck here?"

"Billy asked around, and nobody has any gasoline, not enough to tank a car anyway. So he tried to go up to Highway 90 to get you some himself, but there are trees down and he couldn't get through. The road is completely blocked. The little bridge is under water as well, so there's no going anywhere. We can't even call for help. The phones are down."

"My cell-phone isn't working either. And you don't have any internet, do you?" Margo's spirit plummeted suddenly at the thought. She couldn't take her disappointment out on Josie, who was so nice, but she wanted to scream and scream in frustration. She really, really didn't want to spend a few days in Palmetto Bay, especially without internet.

Josie laughed softly and put a hand on Margo's arm. "I'm sorry that you have to be stuck here, sha. I'm sure you were ready to continue your trip. But I'll be happy to have your company for a few days. Come on, child, smile. You can make the most of it, maybe find something to do. Read, spend some time on the beach, and keep this old gal company. At least we have electricity."

"Yes. True that. I'm grateful for the electricity. I guess I could do a little detecting. Find out more about the castaway, and the famous survivor of the Camilla Star. "

"How come? Are you a private detective?"

"Actually, yes. Thankfully, not for a living, so I get to pick and choose my cases. I take only the very interesting ones."

"Well, *ça c'est bon*. It seems that you showed up at the right time, Miss Margo, because this woman with the black rose tattoo appearing on the beach like that after a storm, that's mighty fishy. It needs to be investigated." She smiled kindly at Margo who couldn't help herself and smiled back.

"There might be a perfectly reasonable explanation, Josie."

"There might be, but somehow I doubt it."

The Body On The Beach

"I'M GOING TO SHOW YOU SOMETHING. I'll be right back." Josie disappeared behind the mirror. When she came back a few minutes later, she was holding a battered cardboard box, the size you would put a pair of boots in. She rummaged among the papers in it and finally picked one up. She handed it to Margo. It was a large photograph in color that should have been framed because of how well it had turned out, and yet it hadn't.

The woman in the photograph was a young Josie, about Margo's age—maybe mid-twenties. She was wearing an emerald green party dress that must have suited her fair complexion beautifully. Next to her, a handsome young man, hard to recognize as her overweight, greasy husband Billy, stood awkwardly, glaring at the camera. Neither of them was smiling.

They were standing in front of a cavernous, oversized fireplace. Above the lintel hung in all its magnificence, the portrait of a surprisingly handsome woman, young, blonde, full of life and full of jewels. On her shoulder, that she had playfully turned toward the painter was the black rose. Just like the shoulder of the young castaway. Josie was right. The young woman on the beach was—at least superficially— very much like the image of Striker Grott's mother Maude, tattoo and all.

"So this was taken in Striker Grott's house."

"*Oui, oui.* That was the last party ever held in the big house. It was Maude's birthday, so Striker Grott went all out. The house was full of flowers. Truckloads of food had been delivered all throughout the day, and the cake, which you can't see in the picture, was the most magnificent cake ever made. Maude was beautiful. She wasn't so young anymore, but she never had lost that fresh, youthful beauty. There wasn't a man in Palmetto Bay that wasn't in love with her.

"Something must have happened the night of that party after everyone left. I don't know. I remember feeling that there was tension between the Grotts, but nothing I could put my finger on. *De toute façon*, Striker Grott never entertained again. Maude and her husband vanished from the town's life. No more parties were held up in the big house. It was sad though because the town depended on him so much financially. The bakery, the florist, all the merchants who helped the Grotts keep their *status quo* suddenly stopped being needed. They went broke and then left town."

"But I thought you still had contact with him."

"I do. Every week I bring him some red wine up to the house, so I've seen Maude's painting many times. Since I buy wine for the pub, I order extra for him. Good for his heart he says. But he's an invalid in a wheelchair and can't come and get it by himself."

"What's wrong with him?"

"He says he has osteoarthritis, but I'm not sure that's true. Somehow he doesn't look that sick to me. But he's an old man. I should say he's a wretched old man. Now that he has a foot in the grave nobody talks bad about him, but there was a time when he was the most hated man around here. I'm surprised nobody ever decided to murder him."

"That bad?"

"Oh yes, and worse. There's talk that like his daddy before him, he killed his wife. There was a handsome gardener and the young Mrs. Grott was lonely. The thing is that there's really nothing to do around here. At least, we all work. We have the fishermen, and there's a small post office, a few restaurants for the locals, a grocery store, and this hotel.

"But poor young Mrs. Grott must have been bored out of her mind. Her husband was always gone on business and she, all alone in that big house by herself. With the gardener. Or so my mother used to say. She found solace in the tempestuous arms of the handsome young man.

"And then apparently Striker Grott came home one day, and he found them together. Well, that's what the idle gossip mongers think, anyway."

"That must have been horrible. Does anyone know what really happened to them?"

"Mais well, the young man was never seen or heard from after that. And mind you, his family was from around here and they got very angry. There had always been rumors that he mistreated his employees, so the town folks assumed that the gardener and young Mrs. Grott had run away, scared of the husband. But the family of the young man wouldn't have it. He would have never left his widowed mother behind like that, they said. They insisted he was murdered. They wanted to lynch Striker Grott. It took the Sheriff and several local men to stop them from going up the hill and finishing the miserable man off. My mother, who insisted she knew it all, told anyone who'd listen that the master had killed them in a jealous rage."

"If he did, he got away with it."

"And now listen to this. This is the really weird part. You've seen Maude Grott's portrait with the black rose on her shoulders, oui?"

"Yes."

"Well, when he got married, he forced his young wife to have the same tattoo made on her shoulder. Besides, she looked very similar in type to his late mother. Honey blonde hair and all that."

"Wow. That does beg quite a few awkward questions."

"Tongues were wagging, my mother says. She heard it from her mother. It was the talk of the town when he brought her home."

Violence And Death

BILLY CLAMBERED OUT OF THE ROTTING sloop and looked at the bloody gash on his arm. Damn. He was getting too old for this. He took his bandana off and wrapped the wound. Infection, for sure. Damn. Josie was going to kill him.

He looked around. That woman Margo was on the shore. That nosy-looking outsider. He didn't like the way she watched them. They were lucky there was no one else on the beach. If they had to, they could easily deal with her. He climbed back down and hollered.

"Nick, Joe? Where are you guys? We have to hurry up."

"What do you want to do with the bodies?" Nick asked.

"I don't know. Let me think." Billy sat down on a piece of rotting wood and put his head in his hands. "Maybe it was a stupid thing to do, to kill them."

"Too late for regrets, man. The deed is done." Nick was nervous and so were the others. They were standing in front of Billy, shivering in their wet clothes, hostile. They were standing knee-deep in water. "We can't just leave the bodies here."

"Well, what else are we going to do? The woman, the outsider, she's standing on the pier watching us. We can't just load the bodies on the boats and bring them. I bet she wants to ask us what we found."

"Yeah, she looks like the nosy type."

"We could get rid of her," one of the guys said, passing his thumb across his neck. "Piece of cake."

"No, we can't, not unless we have no other choice. She's friends with Josie now. She'll ask questions."

"What got into you anyway?" Nick asked Billy. "Why did you have to kill them?"

"I don't know. There were too many of us to share. Besides, Josh came at me first. He had murder in his eyes. All I did was defend myself."

"So you killed Josh too? You're insane, man. I don't want no part of this. I'm getting out of here."

"Nick, be reasonable. There will be more to go around."

"No, Billy. I can't. I didn't sign up for this. You can keep the gold. I don't want it. Josh was my friend." Nick started climbing up the rotten steps and a couple of other guys followed him. They looked fed up as well.

"Where are you going, guys? We are in this together, aren't we?" Billy was up on his feet now. He was opening and closing his massive fists, and his nostrils were flaring like an angry bull's. "You come back here, you hear me? This gets out, and we're all dead."

"This is going to get out. And you know it, Billy. The press is going to arrive, and the coast guard, and all the nosy folks from around here, and they'll come and dive into the wreck and they'll find the bodies."

"No, Nick. I can't let you leave. You'll have a couple of drinks, and you'll tell everyone what happened. Guys, grab 'em."

Billy had too many friends. Nick fought for his life. They were all slipping into the murky water and throwing punches. Any time Nick or one of his friends made it to the deck, someone pulled them back down. Rusty nails and protruding metal scratched at the men as they tried to escape. But Billy and his buddies were determined to keep them down there.

Suddenly, Billy shoved his allies aside. He had a harpoon in his hand. Where he had found it was anyone's guess.

"You bastard," he told Nick. "I thought you were my friend."

Nick looked at Billy, his eyes wide with surprise. Then he saw the harpoon and he started shaking.

"Wait up, Billy," his voice quivered. "What are you doing with that, man?" He backed up, trying to get away, but with every step he kept slipping. Billy had a maniacal smile on his face. Showing his sharp teeth, he grimaced at the pleasure of the kill. When the harpoon entered Nick's soft flesh, Billy sighed with relief. He pushed it all the way in, and then he pulled it back out.

Nick, a trickle of blood running down the side of his mouth, took a step or two. He looked at Billy, shock written all over his face, and then he looked at the wound in his stomach. Blood was gushing from it, and he put his hands on it, trying to keep the blood from flowing away. But it was too late for Nick. He fell on his knees, and still with that look of surprise, he fell down on his side, and within seconds he was dead.

Nick's friends, the ones that had tried to escape, were paralyzed with shock. Billy's friends rounded them up and pushed them into a corner.

"What are we going to do with them?" one of the guys asked.

"Only one thing we can do."

"Come on, Billy, enough killing for one day?"

"Do you have a better idea? If we leave any witnesses alive, we're all dead meat."

The men looked at each other. There were four dead men back in the cargo hold. Now here, there was one more. And Nick's friends, who would surely tell on them if they let them go. They had their treasure, but they had more than they had bargained for. Someone had to get rid of those dead bodies before they started stinking, or before the coast guard arrived.

Pete, Big Pete, stepped out of a dark corner with his big fish gutting knife. He pushed the other guys aside impatiently and approached Nick's friends, who were huddled—terrified—in the corner. He grabbed one of them by the hair and with one well calculated, fluid movement, cut his throat. He threw the dead man on the floor and went for the next one. Pete was an enormous man. He towered over the other fishermen by almost a foot. He was as strong as a bull, too. Nobody would stand up to Pete unless they were skunk drunk. So Pete grabbed Nick's friends, and one by one cut their throats with strong steady strokes as if he had done this many times before.

"Okay, that's solved," he said. "What now?"

Stuck In Town

MARGO WENT TO THE PARKING LOT to check on her car. She passed her hands sadly on a dent or two. Her pretty car. Brooks was going to fuss at her for not taking better care of it.

She looked around at the empty plaza with its circular roundabout and the stone statue of the historic figure watching over it. *Rodrigo Palma*, said the bronze plaque, arguably the founder of Palmetto Bay. She stared listlessly out at the calm blue sea. There was no trace of the terrible storm except for the litter of algae and flotsam on the beach. No more smell of ozone, only the salty fresh ocean breeze. Incoming waves lapped gently at the shore with a soft whoosh. Birds squawked as they flew overhead. Someone was cooking fried fish. She inhaled.

Out there, the dark rotting hull of the shipwreck stuck on the sandbank loomed like a bad omen over the bay. Did it seem to her that it had shifted slightly since the early morning? Josie said it would probably slip back into the water in a few days.

Some of the boats were rowing back already. Had they found anything interesting? She decided to go greet them at the pier and find out.

The fishermen docked and a number of them hopped off the boat. Whatever they had found was covered with tarps. If it was the treasure they were carrying there, why were they so gloomy? A big burly guy stepped out from the group and stuck his hand out.

"Hi, you must be Margo. Josie's told me all about you. I'm her husband Billy."

THE BLACK ROSE RETURNS

"Hi. I saw you at the pub last night. You have blood all over you," she said, and then bit her tongue when she saw the hostile look in Billy's eyes.

"Yes, I cut myself badly." He lifted his arm to show her, and Margo saw it was wrapped in a dirty bandanna. The blood had seeped through. Then Margo squirmed when she saw there was blood splatter on all the guys coming her way on the dock. Instinctively, she nodded at Billy like she hadn't noticed.

"You better clean that well before it gets infected."

"I sure will." The belligerence in his voice dared Margo to say anything else, but she couldn't help herself and it came out anyway.

"Seems like you found something," she said pointing at the bulging tarps. "Anything interesting?"

"Well, you know... can't say yet." Billy's eyes were dead black pools of animosity. "And now, if you would excuse us, Miss." Margo's heart did a skip and she stepped aside to let Billy go. Some of the men followed him toward the pub. One enormous guy, Billy's friend Pete— she was sure—almost pushed her into the water when he aggressively walked by her not even nodding a hello. The other men turned the boats around and rowed away in the direction of the boathouses. When he reached the door to the pub, Billy turned around and looked at her. He was too far to see his face but his body language was contentious and unfriendly. All of a sudden she knew that Billy didn't want her to watch the men row away. She wondered why.

So she looked quickly away. She didn't like this place at all. So far, aside from Josie, not one person had shown any friendliness toward her. Heck, maybe that was why tourism was dead.

There being nothing else to do, Margo turned her attention to the mysterious woman on the beach. She might as well look into that. She went back to her car, took her suitcase out of the trunk, and headed for her room.

Up at the top of the stairs, she was surprised to see that Pepper Paws sat watching her as if waiting for her to come home. Margo giggled. That cat was something. They unpacked the suitcase together, and Pepper had to sniff every new item for approval. Then, the cat threw herself down on the quilt and closed her eyes. Within seconds, she was sleeping, twitching in her dreams, whimpering contentedly.

Margo took stock of her supplies. Computer, check. Internet, no check. Plenty of paper and pens. She never left home without them. So it would be hard to do research. She changed into a cheerful summer dress and sandals and ran back downstairs. For a brief second she wondered if it had been prudent to leave her door ajar for the cat, but then she shrugged and forgot all about it.

Downstairs, Josie was polishing the bar top absentmindedly. She seemed to be troubled about something, but when she saw Margo, she smiled.

"Josie, do you have a public library in town?"

Josie laughed. "You know, Margo, you don't seem to have any idea of how small this town really is. We only have a library of sorts in the old church. We had a priest for a while who was fond of collecting old books. He was a strange one, Father Mike."

"What do you mean by strange?"

"Oh, I don't know. Sometimes I got the feeling that he had no idea what he was doing. Not that I'm an expert Catholic. We've only had priests sporadically. After a while they all seem to get tired of Palmetto Bay and don't come back.

"Mais well, it's no more than a couple of big bookshelves, but there were some handwritten journals, an encyclopedia, that kind of stuff. The priest never comes anymore but he might have left some of the books behind. Do you want to look at them?"

"Oh yes, please."

"*Eh bien,*" Josie told her, "but you can't walk all the way there in those sandals and that pretty dress."

"I'll run upstairs and change."

"Okay. I have the keys to the place. And I think I have a map of the area around here somewhere."

While Margo walked back up the stairs to her room to change, she thought about the colorful scarf Josie was wearing around her neck. And how the scarf was not quite wide enough to cover the greenish-purplish bruise it was trying to hide. Then she remembered noticing the swollen eyelids and the black circles under her eyes as if she had been crying. Josie was a lovely person. She hoped that it wasn't that nasty, burly husband of hers, making her cry.

Her room was empty. The cat was gone. Better this way, she told herself, and prudently locked the door behind her. Downstairs, someone had turned the jukebox on.

The Old Church

MARGO FOLLOWED THE MAP. To get to the church, she had to walk across the deserted one-street town. Perhaps Palmetto Bay had once been a lovely seaside place with potential. Some of the houses had been built with ambition. Some of them were in the Hacienda style, with mock tile roofs and white stucco. Others looked like miniature Plantation homes, with columns holding up balconies of rusting wrought iron. Even the sidewalks had been mapped out wide, with a better future in mind.

Yet, a number of the houses were empty and boarded up. Paint was peeling, and the mildew had made heavy inroads. There were dogs in almost every front yard—many of them cruelly tied up with chains—and for the most part they looked hungry and neglected. Behind the windows of those houses still inhabited, curtains were pulled to the side discreetly as the nosy people of Palmetto Bay watched Margo walk by. This was hostile territory. She knew she was being watched. She could feel it. And it made her feel very uncomfortable.

Every hundred feet or so, side streets opened up off the main one, but they all seemed dead ends. Most of them weren't even paved over but just had a layer of crushed oyster shells thrown on top. It really was a very small town, one that was dying. She walked to the end of the road self-consciously and was relieved when she finally left the town behind.

She took the little sandy trail that headed east, per Josie's instructions. Soon she began to climb a gentle incline. The path had almost disappeared from lack of use. Overgrown, untrimmed bushes and tall grasses scratched at her arms and legs on the way. The church wasn't a popular destination place anymore. It was a shame. The hike was invigorating. Birds twittered happily in the bushes and looked at her with curiosity. Butterflies and lizards scampered in all directions and she walked carefully, making sure not to step on them.

When she reached the clearing, she gasped with joy. What an appropriate place to build a church. It sat on a promontory overlooking the bay. Its graceful dome seemed to be reaching for heaven. She walked to the edge of the cliff crunching the pebbles under her feet. The sun was shining gloriously, warming her hair and her skin. On the horizon, the sea and the cloudless sky met and blended as if they were one. High up, on the top of the cliff, you felt as if heaven was but one touch away. And there at your feet, the world, the sea, and everything good and evil were all left behind.

She watched the waves reach the shore and turn to froth. The sound of the whooshing ebb and flow echoed up to where she stood and she closed her eyes for just a second to breathe in the magnificence of God's creation, feeling the warmth of the sun and the gentle breeze on her face. She wondered about the people in the town below, and the malevolent atmosphere she couldn't help but notice. Had they abandoned the church because they had turned to darker forces, or had the priest stopped coming because of them?

From where she stood, the town was visible at the curve of the bay and she could see her hotel in miniature and some other tiny houses. Out on the sandbank, the shipwreck stood its ground at an angle, its rotting mast hanging like a broken wing. Dozens of little boats came and went busily, those heading back to shore heavy, laden with barrels. It sure seemed like they had found their whiskey.

Leaving speculation for later, Margo turned around to admire the unusual church. Built in aging brownish-red brick, it was not your traditional structure, but it was completely round, like 11th or 12th-century Scandinavian churches. It rose to the sky almost like a lighthouse, crisply delineated against the pristine blue of the afternoon sun. Stained glass windows high above her were protected by heavy chicken wire. The circular, segmented dome must have been copper at one time because it was now greenish and dull. A Lorraine cross topped the dome and reached to heaven as if demanding admittance for the faithful.

It was a lovely church. Shame that in a few years it would become swallowed up by the vegetation around it and people would eventually forget that it ever existed. The gravel underfoot had protected it from the worst of the weeds, but they would eventually take over, as they always did. Soon, ivy creepers would climb up the crumbling, neglected walls and tear into the chicken wire. Once they became strong enough, they would break the precious stained glass and crawl into the sanctuary uninvited, where they would—in a decade or two—overtake the sanctuary completely and decimate the work of art and love that it had once been. And then, nothing would be left but ruins.

She walked around the walls, crunching the oyster shell gravel under her feet, and she touched the rough brick wall with her fingertips. Thank you for not letting me come in sandals, Josie, she thought. It had been rough terrain. A stone bench stood solitary facing Shark Bayou. She imagined herself sitting on that bench and contemplating life and death and the universe.

The main door was massive, the way they don't make them anymore. She inserted the key. The handle turned but the heavily carved gothic wooden door had swelled with the passage of time and the numerous rains and was stuck closed forever. Margo walked around and found a small metal door so rusty and mildewed that it was almost invisible against the red clay bricks. She tried the keys and found one that fit. After some pushing and shoving, it finally budged.

Holding her breath in awe, she stepped into the absolute silence of the circular church and looked around. Light streamed down on her through the stained glass windows in a cascade of colors that shone in rainbows of light and struck the brass of the candle holders and the metal inscriptions at the base of the marble statues. Rows of empty pews stood in line in dusty silence, forgotten by the faithful and carelessly left behind. The sounds of the outside world: the pounding of the waves, the cheering of the Bonaparte Gulls, the branches, and the bushes rustling against each other in the breeze, all that was muted by the heavy walls.

THE BLACK ROSE RETURNS

The twelve Stations of the Cross in the stained glass stared down at her from narrow windows telling her the story of the suffering and death of Christ.

The sanctuary had been suspended in a moment in time. She approached quietly the rose-colored marble altar and the statue of Jesus on the crucifix hanging on the wall behind it. She couldn't believe that they had left everything behind. Brass candleholders stood dulled and unpolished. Even a large bible stood open on a carved wooden stand, its pages curled backward with age and humidity. Even the altar cloth, lovingly hand-embroidered with gold threads, had been left behind. This was insane. If the priest had quit, surely he wouldn't have abandoned these precious things so cavalierly.

She stepped down from the altar and walked around. The old fashioned wooden pews were elaborately carved in the first three rows and plain wood further on. That was where the rich people once sat, on the fancy ones, and further down, the commoners. As she looked back toward the altar, she admired the ornate lectern, elevated above a handful of steps, and a small organ to the right.

She walked to the entrance of the church, to the front door, the one that was impossible to open. It was completely in darkness. Almost hidden by a column, a tight circular stairway led upward, seemingly nowhere. Testing the rungs one by one for possible rot, she headed upstairs, not trusting the banister completely. She was surprised to enter a large, well lit circular room, invisible to the outside world. She was under the dome, above the sanctuary, above the stained glass.

A very large, very wide window overlooked the sea and the slowly darkening sky. She was way high up. She couldn't see the little town from here, but the shipwreck was clearer than ever. The seas were getting rough, and for a minute or two, she watched the fishermen heading for shore again. It would probably be wise to hurry up and then head back to the Drunken Duck unless she wanted to spend the night up here. She shivered at the thought.

She quickly examined the upstairs, and found it to contain the one large room that also served as a bedroom, a bathroom, and a kitchenette, and off to one side, an office with a window that overlooked the back of the church and part of the water. It was getting dark now in the room and she saw herself faintly reflected in the office window. But that was not all she saw. The desk was facing her and the door as she had entered. But the swivel office chair was turned away from the door toward the window, and someone dressed in black was sitting in it silently as if looking out to sea.

The hairs stood up on the back of Margo's neck as she felt a moment of irrational fear. She clasped her hands to her mouth to suppress the scream coming up from her lungs. Controlling the urge to flee, she took a step toward the figure. *Hello,* she said a number of times with a squawking voice, wildly aware that she sounded like a goose.

When she got no answer and no movement, she grasped her throat as a terrible foreboding shook through her. She took a couple of steps and turned the swivel chair around with a shaking hand. There was a figure slumped in it all right. Terrified, she tried to look away when she realized what it was, but it was too late. She'd seen it all right. It was the body of a priest, or what was left of him, still wearing his soutane. A huge knife was sticking out of his chest. He hadn't abandoned his parishioners after all. This must be the priest that never came back. And now she knew why.

The Pub And The Locals

SHE WALKED SLOWLY DOWN THE PATH, considering from all angles the complicated situation she was in. She had no friends in this town other than Josie and calling Josie a friend was a bit of a stretch. She knew how insular and tight-knit small towns could be, and how hostile to strangers. If she was back home, she would call her buddy Sam Stark at the Police Station right away. Here, she wasn't even sure she should mention the priest at all. Weighing her pros and cons, she decided to do a little detecting first. She would come back in the morning with camera, voice recorder and her Glock, and see what she could find.

Unpleasant little place, this town, she told herself. Out in the middle of nowhere, it seemed like such a sleepy, harmless place and yet, a shipwreck from the past, a mysterious woman on the sandy beach, an old man who could or could not be a murderer, a number of possible dead bodies and now a dead priest in a forgotten church, had all managed to intersect themselves into her life on the spot, uninvited.

She fought the vegetation and the darkness that was coming faster now and finally made it to the main street. She hurried down the slope. It seemed like the hotel was farther away than she remembered. And the streets were completely empty. Where was everybody, anyway?

An unseen hostility seemed to follow her like a hungry ghost, and she picked up the pace. A gust of air whistled by her and stirred up dead leaves as she went. She remembered how earlier on, curtains had flickered as she walked by. A lot of curiosity, and yet nobody had bothered to open their doors and say hello. The street lights flickered and did nothing to quell her anxiety. Dogs barked and the wind howled.

She finally opened the double doors to the pub, happy—and so relieved—to be back, and sat down at what was now her usual spot. Pepper Paws was at her designated spot, at the end of the shiny bar top. When she saw Margo, she quickly got up and trotted across the bar to get to her. She greeted Margo as if they had known each other forever.

She watched the locals drink their beer and shell their peanuts from the wall to wall mirror behind the bar. Some people were having dinner. Billy was at a far table with some rough looking friends. They whispered intently while they nursed their beers. The big guy, the really big one who almost shoved her off the dock, he was there too, staring at her with angry eyes. *What was his problem?*

Josie came out of the kitchen behind the bar and greeted her like an old friend.

"Did you find it?" she asked. Her scarf had slipped and the angry marks on her neck were very visible now.

"Josie, you might want to adjust your scarf," Margo told her. She leaned over the bar counter and discreetly helped Josie adjust her scarf. "There," she said. "It's good now."

Josie's hand flew to the scarf, and she seemed to want to say something, and she briefly looked at her customers, but there were too many people watching. Her face was flushed and there was a hint of panic in her eyes. She chose to look at her hands instead, and she wiped the bar counter vigorously and unnecessarily.

"Yes, actually I did find it," Margo said, trying to sound quite natural. "Lovely place. Didn't have time to look for the books though, because it got dark too soon. May I keep the keys another day?"

"*Mais oui*, of course. It's not like I need them for anything." Josie laughed her throaty laugh, but tonight it sounded hollow. Her hand went up to her neck and again she adjusted the scarf. Then she looked away self-consciously. Margo really liked her. She tried to smile at Josie, but she was terribly sad. Those ugly marks on Josie's throat could have only come from Billy.

Josie excused herself and stepped away to serve some patrons at the other end of the bar. Meantime, someone cranked up the jukebox in the corner and the toe-tapping rhythm of a Cajun two-step filled the room. Some people got up and danced. Margo stared at them. This was probably what they did every single day of their lives: come to the pub and drink and then go dance. It was a time loop continuum, where every day was a carbon copy of the one before. She realized she was staring, and she looked away.

"Is the woman conscious yet?" she asked Josie who was back at polishing the counter.

"They say she is. But they won't let anyone bother her yet. Too soon, they said."

"Bummer. So nobody has heard her story."

"I guess not. But the postman, um, that's Benjamin Stoops, he said he went to deliver some mail at the infirmary, and they told him the young woman is saying that she belongs on the Camilla Star."

"But that's preposterous." Margo rolled her eyes.

"That's what I said, but apparently, she knows things about the sloop and the cargo and the people traveling on it that she shouldn't know. She has some people convinced."

"She's faking. That's obvious. But why bother?"

"That's what I told Billy. It makes no sense. But it's early yet. We have to wait until she's allowed to get up and walk around, and then they will let us talk to her. I have to say it's quite intriguing."

"Surely you don't believe it?"

"*Mais non*, not really. But Margo, you have to admit it's strange. She knows the Camilla Star was a pirate ship in disguise."

"You knew it too. All she had to do was a little research."

"But she knows about the treasure. And the slaves, and the survivor."

"So? She must have read the survivor's diary, just like you did."

"I guess. But the survivor also mentions in his journals that there was a mysterious traveler on board. And he suspected it was a young woman. And this woman knew about that too."

Josie and Margo became quiet, and each got lost in their own thoughts. Above the music coming from the jukebox, and above her own thoughts, she could hear clearly the excitement generated by the salvaging of the whiskey barrels. That was all the patrons were talking about. Other things they had come across like china, jars of oils, and kitchen stuff, were all unimportant and had been left behind. The fishermen were mostly excited about the whiskey. So far, dozens of barrels had been recovered in good condition. The rest of the horde could wait forever as far as they were concerned. About the chests of gold coins, nobody breathed a word. Not a one.

"Billy is bringing a barrel to the pub later on tonight. We'll open it here and get to taste the whiskey for ourselves." The locals heard her and cheered.

"In the meantime, where is the infirmary?"

"It's the third street to the right. Back at the dead end."

"I'm going to look in on our mysterious stranger, see if they let me have a word with her."

"Be careful," Josie told her, surprising her with her palpable fear. "It's gotten dark out there."

Before she closed the door behind her, Margo looked back. Josie continued to polish the bar top with feigned enthusiasm, and Pepper Paws stared at her as if she was worried. In the back of the bar, sitting in their usual place, Billy and his gigantic pal Pete whispered. Billy's fist was closed. He struck the table angrily and one of the beer bottles toppled over. She quietly let the door go.

The Woman With The Tattoo

THE NIGHT WAS HOT AND UNPLEASANT. Muggy. The sun had all but disappeared, except for the tinge of dying yellow and red lights on the horizon as another dazzling Louisiana sunset put itself to bed. Crickets, sensing rain, were chirping up a storm. Flying things like moths and such, circled around the halo of the street lights and occasionally banged against them with a sizzling sound as they got burned. Dogs bared vicious fangs and barked at her as she walked by. In Palmetto Bay, it was a night probably like any other one. She shivered.

It wasn't that Margo really wanted to go to the infirmary. It was that she didn't want to sit in the pub until she got sleepy. She was restless. She was out of her element: small room, no phone, no internet, nothing interesting to read, but mostly—except for Josie—such an unfriendly place. Anything had to be better than watching people get drunk in the pub.

Margo hastened down the deserted main street by the light of the flickering lamps with her hands in her pockets. A cool wind whistled by her as it came up from the water, picking up dead leaves and discarded pieces of paper. It was almost chilly, and she regretted not having a jacket, but she had no interest in turning back.

Her footsteps echoed in the empty street, or so she imagined. From the corner of her eyes she could see the multidirectional shadows she cast about her as she walked. They gave her a creepy feeling, those long dark shadows that walked with her, and she kept turning her head to see if she was being followed.

She avoided the storm debris and the piles of soggy leaves. There was flotsam and dead stuff everywhere. People hadn't bothered cleaning it up. It was beginning to stink too. Mosquitos buzzed about her eyes and ears, and she swept them aside over and over again, but they wouldn't leave her alone. She couldn't find one good thing about this town.

Margo turned where Josie had told her, third street to the right, and walked in almost total darkness toward the bluish neon light that called for the sick to come forth, like a beacon in the night. The pavement was torn up in places, and she kept stumbling on tufts of weeds. Undomesticated rose bushes, reaching out from behind chicken wire fences, scratched her as she walked by them. Still, it was probably safer than walking in the middle of the street. Not that there was anyone out driving.

The radio was on in the infirmary. She heard it before she pushed the glass doors open. It almost startled her after the total silence out there. An unsmiling young nurse behind the front desk looked up from her magazine. The place was so brightly lit that even her skin looked paper white. She looked strict and unwilling to give in an inch.

"Hi. My name is Margo Fontaine. I'm staying at the Drunken Duck until they clear the road."

"I know who you are."

"Really?"

"Everyone knows who you are. How can I help you?"

"I was hoping to talk to the young woman who washed ashore this morning."

"Sorry. Doctor said she needs to be left alone."

"Please let me talk to her," she asked again. "Just for a few minutes. If she gets tired of me, I promise to leave right away."

"Oh, all right. Let me ask her if she's up to it." Margo followed her down a long and empty hallway.

"Has she said anything?"

"Only that she doesn't remember what happened."

"Is she from around here?"

"I don't think so. I was born here, and I've never seen her before. Wait here."

Margo stopped at the end of the hallway in front of a closed door and waited for a few minutes. The place was as clean as a whistle and way too nice for a place like Palmetto Bay. The young castaway must have been the only patient in the infirmary. Hers was the only closed door. Finally, the nurse came back out and held the door open for her.

The woman sitting up in the bed was about her own age, around twenty-five. She had long honey blonde hair that was carelessly up in a chignon. A lock of hair had fallen back on her eyes, and she swept it away gracefully. Someone had given her a pair of men's striped pajamas. She looked good in them.

"Hi. My name is Margo Fontaine. I liked your nightgown better," she told the young woman as she pulled up a chair and sat by the bed.

"They washed it for me. It is hanging in the armoire. How did you know?"

"I saw you on the beach, lying on the sand. You look good for someone who almost drowned."

"I am doing fine. Except for my head. It hurts." She leaned forward guilelessly and parted her hair. Margo could see an ugly lump on her scalp.

"Yikes. It looks bad."

"They said I have a con something," she said and smiled shyly.

"That must be a concussion." She smiled back. You couldn't help but like the young castaway. She had a very friendly smile. Margo wondered what she was up to.

"My name is Jeanne." She looked down at her hands and examined them absentmindedly. "But that's all I remember." She looked up with clear blue eyes that seemed incapable of deception.

"Do you remember how you got here at least?"

"Only that there was a storm. No, wait. The sea was rough. I remember I was very scared." Jeanne's eyes got glazed over as if she were watching the events on a screen. "They told me to stay in my cabin because it was safer, so I stayed. Then the Captain came in and tried to grab me. I pushed him away. He said he was trying to save me, but I did not believe him. He tried again, and I pushed him out of the cabin and locked the door.

"Then the storm got worse and nobody was coming to save me, so I opened the door and looked outside. There was nobody there. They were all gone. They had left me behind. Maybe the Captain was trying to save me after all. I held on to the rigging but the waves kept getting bigger and bigger. The sky was black, and the storm was so loud that I wanted to cover my ears, but I was scared to let go of the rigging.

"I held on for a while, but I could not fight the waves any longer. Then something hit me on the head, and I fell and slipped. Then the darkness came. It was terrible, the darkness. And it was very cold. I tried to hold my breath, but I couldn't. My lungs were about to explode. So I breathed in the saltwater, and it burned my throat, and it burned in my lungs like fire, and then nothing. It felt like the darkness had lasted forever, but then I opened my eyes and I was in this strange place and in this strange room. That is all I remember."

Jeanne had become breathless telling her story. Her chest heaved as if it were fighting the burning sensation in her lungs all over again. There was panic in her big blue eyes. She looked so sincere. How on earth did she do it? And why?

"How about the rose on your shoulder?"

"The black rose?"

"Yes. How did you get it?"

"We all had one."

"Who's *we*?"

"The girls. We were all stolen from our families and taken to Martinique by ship. Then this horrible little fat man with a funny hat took us to his house. They made us take our shirts off and they branded us with a hot iron."

"So it's not a tattoo?"

"You mean a *tattaw*? No, it is not. Look." Jeanne opened the top button of her striped pajama and slipped it over the shoulder. She turned to the side.

"Can I touch it?"

"Of course you may. It does not hurt anymore."

Margo passed her fingertips over the rough edges of the black rose. They felt like they had been carved into the young woman's flesh with a rough knife. Her stomach lurched. It must have caused a horrendous pain. She was baffled beyond words.

"Is that all you remember? Do you remember the name of your ship?"

"Yes of course. The Camilla Star."

"And the other passengers?"

"Yes. There was the Captain and there were many sailors. I do not know their names. There was also my friend Mark."

"Hold on, your friend Mark?"

"Yes. Mark Driskoll. But he is a proper friend. I have known him for many years, from before I was kidnapped. I was very surprised to see him on the same ship. Then there were many slaves in the cargo hold. They cried all the time. They wanted to be let out, but the Captain told the sailors not to open their hatch."

"I thought slavery was abolished a long time ago."

"It was abolished before my mother was born, but the plantation owners did what they wanted anyway. My master, the one who had me branded, had many slaves. He was ordered to let them go free, so he sold them quickly to get some of his money back. I was also sold."

"Really?"

"Oh yes. We were all sold to the Man On The Hill."

"What man on the hill?"

"I don't know that. Everyone called him the Man On The Hill."

"What else do you remember?"

"Oh, the monkey. Where's the monkey? Is it all right?"

"What monkey?" Margo felt like this was getting more and more bizarre. "Was there a monkey on board?"

"Why, yes. Maddock, the Captain's pet monkey."

Margo stared at the young woman, baffled, but fully aware that there was a con game going down somewhere. But what was it? The young woman seemed so sincere, so friendly, and so shy. What on earth was she up to?

Gloria

MARGO HATED GOING STRAIGHT BACK to the hotel. It was too early to go to bed, and she was too restless to sleep anyway.

She left behind the brightly lit area by the infirmary door and stepped into the gloomy penumbra. The air was sticky with the salty moisture. It smelled like rain, and a soft rumbling coming from the clouds hinted at an impending storm. Once she left the sounds of the radio behind, the silence became absolute. The decaying houses on both sides of the street sat—like in a black and white movie or an abandoned film set—staring at her with their windows dark like blind eye sockets.

She walked fast to the main street, more than happy to leave the creepy, empty houses behind. When she got to the corner, she looked around and saw what she had missed earlier that night, the police station, right across the street from the infirmary, on the other side of the street.

Even though her sense of self-preservation told her to go back to the hotel, her feet walked across the street and planted themselves in front of the station. It was a small building with a big important sign that said Palmetto Bay Police Department. The entrance had been cleared of storm debris already. There was a light on inside, and she questioned one last time whether she was ready to tell the story of the dead priest or not.

It was not an easy decision. Initially she had considered doing some detecting first, but the right thing was to tell the police what she had found. But doing so could put her in personal danger. She knew well enough how law enforcement worked, especially in small, narrow-minded communities. They could throw her in jail and keep her there until they slowly figured out that the man had obviously been dead for a very long time before she ever got there. How long would that take? A week? A month? Would they even let her make a phone call?

Before she could regret it, she pushed the door open and walked up to the front desk where a woman in uniform was reading a book. She looked up at Margo but did not smile.

"Hello," she said. Then she waited.

Margo, determined to make a new friend, gave the woman a grin.

"Hello. My name is Margo Fontaine. I blew into town with the storm yesterday. Now I'm stuck here until they clear the road."

"I know who you are. How may I help you?" Margo got closer and took a peek at the book.

"Good book?" she asked, trying to break the ice.

"Yes, very. How may I help you?" She repeated.

"Oh, nothing. I was just walking by and I thought I'd come in and say hello. I ended up in Palmetto Bay because I kind of got lost."

"Where were you heading?"

"Cypremort Point. I was going to meet a friend for a few days at the beach."

"It will be days before they clear the road. You might as well make yourself comfortable. Our beach is prettier than Cypremort Point's anyway."

"Have you seen the shipwreck?"

"Yes, but not officially."

"What do you mean?"

"Simply that if I admitted that there's a shipwreck, I would have to radio the Coast Guard. I have an uncle who's a fisherman. As you can probably see, this is a very poor community. We desperately need money to keep the town going so, if they find some gold, it will be good for all."

"Don't worry about me keeping the secret. Josie at the pub explained already, so I promise never to tell."

"Thank you for that. So how can I help you?"

"You keep asking me that, and I don't know where to begin." Margo stood in front of the desk squirming and twisting her hands. "Can I buy you a cup of coffee?"

"I'd say it's kind of late in the day for coffee."

"Then a drink? Please? I have to talk to a police officer. Someone I can trust."

"And how do you know that you can trust me?"

"Well I don't, but I still need a policeman."

"All right then. I'll be happy with a beer. We could sit outside on a bench by the water and have some privacy. Give me a minute. My partner's off somewhere, so I have to lock up."

Gloria and Margo strolled toward the pub in silence. Down at the end of the slope, the waters of Shark Bayou shimmered in the moonlight. Some of the houses on their way had finally had their lights turned on, and the sounds of family life filtered out of them. The air down by the water got cool at night, and a breeze came whistling up from the bay and made Margo shiver.

Gloria was an imposing woman. She was tall and slender, with long auburn hair held in a ponytail. Her bangs covered her eyebrows and made her look young in the street light, and yet Margo had the feeling that Gloria had lived long and hard. However, she looked like she had been born to wear a police uniform. Her belt jingled with official paraphernalia as she walked with a steady, self-confident pace, and she had a gun. She looked like a dangerous woman. She never cracked a smile.

They sat with their beers, staring out at the water. The tight little waves splashed on the beach and played with each other before slipping back. She fidgeted with her beer mug while she wondered how she was going to bring up the subject of the dead priest in front of a complete stranger. Finally, it was Gloria who talked.

"You did say you wanted to discuss something."

"Yes, yes. But it's always iffy when you find a dead body, and you don't have friends in the police department, so I don't know where to begin." Margo's hand went up to her mouth, and she quickly looked at Gloria when she realized what she had just said.

"You mean you found a dead body? Is that what you've been trying to tell me?"

"Umm, yes. I found it up at the church on the cliff."

"The church?" Gloria looked at Margo with her eyes wide open with surprise. It was obviously the last thing she expected to hear. "Are you serious?"

"Yes, I am."

"And what were you doing up there?"

"I was bored and thinking about all the days I was going to be cooped up here because of the trees down and the flooded bridge, so I thought I'd look into some strange occurrences on request from Josie, and there's no public library, so Josie said that the few books about the history of the town are up in the church. So she gave me the keys, and I went to check the place out. The stairs are well hidden behind the statuary. I almost missed them. So I went upstairs, and there are a room, a bathroom, and a little office. I think I found the missing priest, Gloria. And I don't know what to do about it."

"Did you say the missing priest?"

"Yes. I would have normally called my friends at the Palmetto Bay police station, but here, I don't know anyone. I can't really go and tell Josie. The thing is that there's something very wrong."

"What's that?"

"The priest was murdered."

"And how would you know that?"

"He has a knife sticking out of his chest."

"Oh, my God!" Suddenly, Gloria jumped up from the bench as if someone had pulled her up. Her hand was at her throat and her eyes bulged, and she looked like she was about to faint. Her beer mug plopped on a patch of grass in front of the bench and the beer splashed all over her uniform.

"What is it, Gloria? Did you know him?" Margo stepped up to the woman and grabbed her to help steady her.

"I can't be sure. I mean, I used to go to church there, so he must be the same priest. Are you sure it was a priest?"

"Yes. At least I think so. He's wearing a soutane."

"Yes, I guess you're right. He always wore his soutane."

"So I need you to come with me to the church tomorrow, and we have to decide what to do. He was murdered."

"Yes, I realize that. You said that already."

"What should we do?"

"We can't do anything right now. It's dark already. I can arrange to get off early tomorrow, and we can go see."

Margo went back to the pub and got refills for the spilled beer. If she was pale and shaking, nobody noticed. On her way out, Pepper Paws followed her to the beach and jumped up on the bench between them. They all sat quietly for a while watching the waves splash on the sand and then when Margo turned toward Gloria, she saw by the flickering street lamp that she was crying quietly.

"Gloria," she said, putting a hand on the woman's arm. "What's wrong? Why are you crying?"

"I'm not crying." Gloria wiped the tears away with the back of her hand, but they kept coming.

"Of course you are. I can see the tears flowing like floodwater. What's wrong?"

"I knew the priest. At least if he's the one I'm thinking of. I thought he had left without me."

"I don't understand."

"I know. The priest and I, we knew each other from the army. That was a lifetime ago. We went overseas, and we were both lucky to come back alive. Too lucky, if you ask me. I saw things there that will haunt my dreams until the day I die." Gloria passed her hand in front of her eyes as if trying to wipe away the horrors of war. She was looking out at the dark waters, lost in her memories. "Of the thousands that went with us, only a handful returned. Maybe I was not cut out for that life. I don't know. But I took it very hard. Without Mike, I'm sure I would have killed myself. Walked in front of an enemy tank, or something. Mike understood. He too was torn apart by the horror and suffering and—my God—the dust. You wouldn't believe how much dust there was. It got in your eyes, and your nose, and in your mouth, in between your teeth. Imagine, Margo. Dust and dead bodies everywhere. Starving stray dogs eating the dead bodies. Flies buzzing around them. It was unspeakable. At night, Mike and I comforted each other the best we could. And every morning we went back out and faced certain death all over again. But we just kept surviving. We just kept going back to camp at night, when all we wanted was to die.

"So, when we came back to the States, we moved here. I have relatives in Palmetto Bay, and Mike had no family. I came first, to check things out and saw that the old priest had died. So I told him, pretend to be a priest and come and live here. And he did. Mike was a smart man, he read books and familiarized himself with the liturgy, and he came down and moved into the church dome upstairs. Nobody knew of the apartment, and I guess nobody cared to befriend him, which was perfect, because Mike suffered from PTSD, and he needed silence and peace. He would have never been able to integrate into civilian life anyway."

"So that's why Josie said he made mistakes."

"Yes. He did a good job, but he wasn't a real priest so he did mess up sometimes. People thought he was unconventional, is all."

"Then what happened?"

"Imagine when we found out there were living quarters upstairs. It was ideal. He could live up there and explore the beaches in private. People only expected to see him once a week, and his soutane was the perfect disguise. If he occasionally met someone while walking around in a bathing suit or rowing out with diving gear, I mean this is what people do around here. We get tourists once in a while, so it was the perfect setup. Nobody ever questioned it. And I had him near me. I had a place where to come visit him. All I had to do was walk.

"And we were happy. But then, one day, he disappeared. I went to the church and he wasn't there. I looked for him everywhere. Then I went again and again, and that was it. Mass on Sundays stopped. People went up to the church a few times looking for him, but after a while, they gave up. They stopped looking for him. I assumed that he had had an underwater accident while diving, or he had left. Actually, I thought he had left."

"Why? He doesn't sound like the kind of person who would have left you behind."

"Because he started having paranoid delusions. He was convinced that someone was following him. We did occasionally get hunted like animals over there, and many of us were captured and tortured and thrown to the hungry dogs, so I knew what it felt like. So, maybe I wasn't so surprised when he vanished."

"It would seem then that—at some point in time—he came back and dressed up as a priest again, perhaps with the idea of slipping back into his role, but something or someone caught up with him and killed him."

"Yes. That's what it looks like. Thank you for telling me, Margo."

"We still don't know it's him, though."

"I think I know in my heart that it's him." Gloria bent her head and put it in her hands. Margo held her while she sobbed, and patted her back soothingly like you would a crying child. After a while, Gloria got herself together, and without another word, got up and left. All Margo could do was watch her walk away.

Pepper Paws whined and complained trying to get her attention, and when Margo looked down, she saw that the cat was playing with something that had fallen on the sand. She bent down and picked it up. Two little white beads strung together with a small piece of filigree chain. She too had gone to church all her life and knew right away what it was. Part of a broken rosary.

Upstairs in her hotel room, Pepper Paws jumped familiarly on the bed and stretched out, and Margo walked to the window without turning her lights on. Some of the moonlight was shining on the sleeping bay adding that magic touch to the mysteriously silent outdoors that only the moon can. The neon welcome light from the hotel cast a halo of ever-diminishing light beyond the parking lot, out to a stretch of sandy beach where a soft drizzle was falling. She watched for a few minutes the shimmering water reflecting the wedge of moon and the occasional twinkling star. She imagined the threatening hulk of the sloop and the mast, still there, still broken, looming in the penumbra like the stuff that nightmares are made of. Rotting cloths hanging from masts that should have disintegrated decades ago. The wood of the hull—impossibly intact—and a castaway with a fantastic story that made no sense.

Downstairs, close to the bench where she and Gloria had talked earlier about her dead priest, two men had walked out of the pub and were carrying on a heated argument. The bigger one pushed the other one. His body language was so intimidating that it made Margo flinch. Her first impulse was always to go do something, but she knew better than to interfere, though. A stranger in a strange, unfriendly land must not butt in. She drew her curtains and turned the table lamp on.

She checked her phone for the hundredth time and saw that there was still no signal. She desperately wished she could get in touch with home. There was nothing more to do but continue reading *The Moonstone* for a while and then get in bed and sleep.

That night she dreamed with a monkey in a circus outfit and a red fez hat climbing the tall mast of a sloop, and a young woman with weeds tangled in her hair, floating on the salty water, dressed in a long white flowing robe. It was a crazy dream. She snuggled with Pepper, who purred comfortingly, and slept on.

Daisy, Daisy

DAISY WAS RESTLESS AND MISERABLE. Shoes in hand, she walked along the dark and deserted beach wondering where the young woman had come ashore. Not that it mattered, not really. In the silence of the humid, heavy night, the swooshing of the waves sounded loud and deep as they struck the sand, running all the way up to her feet and in between her toes. She wanted to scream at the ship sitting like a rotting hulk out there. She hated it. She wanted to burn the whole thing down and burn the castaway down with it.

There was a bitter taste in her mouth that would not go away. She wished there was someone she could talk to. At first she thought of her mom. But her mom wouldn't understand. What did she know about broken hearts and disappointments? She wiped the raindrops out of her face while she plotted murder. She had never even as much as plucked a chicken. How was she going to murder a human being? But how else could she stop the girl from intruding in her life and ruining everything?

What if she murdered the old man instead? He was the one causing all the trouble after all. Daisy, Daisy, would you do it? Could you do it? All of a sudden, a smug smile spread across her unhappy face. Oh, yes. She definitely could.

Day Three

Tree Down

NINA SIMONE WAS SINGING *Another Woman* on a scratched LP, and the smell of percolating coffee filled the stairwell as Margo and Pepper hopped down the stairs and burst into the kitchen where Josie was singing to herself while making breakfast.

> *But the other woman will always cry herself to sleep*
> *The other woman will never have his love to keep*
> *And as the years go by, the other woman*
> *Will spend her life alone*

"Good morning, Margo. Good morning, Pepper Paws. Pretty day, today, isn't it?" She seemed in an excellent mood. The uncovered bruise on her throat was beginning to fade. "I feel so much better today," she said when she noticed Margo staring at it. "I've made peace with Billy. He apologized last night."

"I don't know much about these things, Josie, but aren't you worried he'll do it again?"

"Maybe he won't anymore. He's had a hard life, you know, and he lets the anger build up inside. Then he drinks to drown his anger, which makes it worse. That's when he lashes out. But now that there's plenty of gold that will solve our financial problems, he won't have any reason to be angry anymore."

She brought two steaming hot café au laits over to a table by the window and they sat down to chat. The LP ran down and it crackled for a minute or two before the arm whirred back to the first song and Nina Simone began singing again.

"Today's the day," Josie said. "They're pulling the gold out. They are working against time. Billy says we probably have today and maybe another day before the coast guard and the reporters arrive. A cruise ship sailed by yesterday afternoon along Shark Bayou. Someone on deck surely must have seen the shipwreck and posted a picture of it online. We can't keep it a secret forever." Josie happily sipped her coffee.

Margo, glad to see Josie in such good spirits, decided not to say anything about the tarp-covered boats. She was pretty sure—given their secretive attitudes—that the fishermen had found more than they were saying already, and whatever they were going back to the ship for was something else. But she smiled at Josie anyway.

"So they found the Captain's quarters then?"

"Yes. Billy peeked in and saw gold coins and jewels spilling out of chests. Today they're going to break the door down and get inside."

"Isn't that dangerous? You told me that the ship could slip back into the sea at any time. They could get trapped in there." The fishermen coming back to shore yesterday had blood all over their clothes. "Or someone could get hurt," she added.

"Oh, I hope not. It has slipped back some, but it is still mostly above water. It will probably hold until the next storm, although you never know about these things. But they are very careful. They know what they're doing."

Before anything else, Margo wanted to check on the tree down and headed south-east, following the main road. After leaving the town behind, the road took her steadily uphill. While she did enjoy the sunshine filtering through the branches of the giant oak trees, all she could think of was getting out of Palmetto Bay.

She found the roadblock about two miles up, a mile after having left the last house behind. The long line of centenarian trees went on forever, but it was not something you noticed when you were driving. Here, standing in the middle of the blacktop, looking up, Margo as small and as insignificant as a speck of sand, the trees seemed to reach to the sky. They were teeming with life, too. If you stood quietly and watched, you could see the squirrels jumping from branch to branch. Blue jays chirped as they bullied other birds and each other, and bugs just buzzed all over the place.

The gigantic trees looked powerful enough to outlive her generation, yet one of them had fallen and was lying right across the road, dying already. Its massive trunk was as thick as she was high. Even climbing over it would have been impossible. The tangled branches of the fallen tree spread out like the hair of a colossal sleeping woman. Nests had been shattered and abandoned, and Margo felt a terrible sadness for all the little critters that had lost their home.

To her right, the roots stuck up from the black soil and went on forever. Margo got close and saw that a long line of fire ants was steadily marching into the shrubbery carrying their eggs, or whatever those little white things were. The leaves were already brown and yellow and brittle. It was obvious that heavy equipment would be needed to clear this mess. And she wouldn't be able to drive around it either, not even if she had a jeep or a pickup. There was simply no clearing wide enough to the other side. So she was trapped, but she knew that already. She wanted to bang on the tree trunk with her fists or to kick it, she was so desperate to get out of there.

Grumpy and frustrated, and having nothing else to do on what promised to be another excruciatingly long day, Margo went back down to the pub. Pepper Paws sat up when she saw her enter and complained loudly, probably because she had been left behind. Josie, elated like a schoolgirl in love was smiling to herself and washing glasses at the bar sink. She told Margo that there was someone waiting for her.

There was only one person in the establishment, so Margo approached the table where one lonely woman sat out by the last window sipping on some hot beverage that was still steaming.

She greeted the woman with a friendly hello and sat down. Josie yelled over a W*ould you like some coffee*? And Margo nodded and looked at the woman sitting across from her. She was probably in her late thirties, frumpy and unattractive. Her hair was untidily up in a bun, and on putting on her cardigan, she had missed a button. Sweat stains under her armpits and around her neck made it obvious that she was nervous.

"Miss Margo, right? Private Detective?"

"Yes, that's me. And who are you, if I may ask?"

"My name is Daisy. I work for Master Grott up in the big house. We was wondering if you could come up for a short visit."

"I would love to come. Would you like to tell me what Mr. Grott wants to see me about?

"I don't know if I should say."

"You might as well, so I can be prepared."

"I guess. You see, there is this young man as works for Master Grott. He does the yard and cleans around the swamp, cuts firewood, that sort of stuff. At noon, he came home with this strange story. There is a shipwreck."

"I know. Have you seen it?"

"Yes, I saw it with my eyes just now."

"And?"

"Well, and so they found this young woman on the beach, yes?"

"Yes, they did."

"And so John tells Master Grott this woman has a tattoo on her shoulder. The tattoo of a black rose. Is that true, Miss?"

"Yes, I know about that too. I've seen it myself. I met the young lady last night but I also saw her lying on the sand after the storm."

"So the black rose is real?"

"Yes, it is. She showed it to me herself. But it's really not a tattoo. She told me she got branded. I've never seen anyone branded before, but this looks terrible. It looks as if someone had cut the rose into her flesh."

"Well, Master Grott wanted the young lady to come and convalesce in the house. So he told John, the man who works for him, to go get her first thing today."

"Really? And why would he want to do that?"

"I'm sure I don't know. Maybe he feels lonely, or maybe he thinks she'll be more comfortable there."

"So, tell me Daisy, why are you so troubled?"

"Well, there's a painting of a woman over the fireplace in the main hall. The woman has a black rose tattooed on her shoulder."

"Yes, I've heard. What of it?"

"Now Master Grott wants the young woman to come and live in the house."

"And this bothers you?"

"Yes, Miss. It bothers me very much. I warned Master Grott that nothing good would come out of it. But I don't know why."

"You still haven't told me why Mr. Grott wants to see me."

"Well, it seems like he found out that you've talked to her, Miss, and he would like to know what you think about her."

"Why would he care what I think?"

"He's heard you're a detective. Is all I can think."

Margo and the woman sat in her little Honda and headed out. One of the side streets opened into a small car trail and started winding up the hill.

"Tell me something, Daisy. Does this road lead to the main highway? I'm stuck in town because of the blocked road."

"No, Miss. It only leads to the house and back. If you want to leave town, you'll have to wait until they get rid of the tree."

Sitting in the passenger car next to a very silent and very grumpy driver, Margo had plenty of time to look around. At times, as the trail twisted and turned, she could see the mast of the broken sloop, and the boats, tiny like models on a toy scenery, rowing back and forth. She wondered if the fabled treasure had been found already. She had two questions, though. The first one was, if they were just picking up the treasure now, what was under the tarps the other day? And if they had been trying to hide the treasure, why were they going back today?

Upon the hill an old yellow house sat alone, standing guard over the seaside. It had once been a beautiful southern plantation home, a grand white-pillared building with a raised red brick foundation, but now it just seemed sad and neglected.

"Does Mr. Grott have any children?" she asked.

"I'm afraid not. No family left either."

"So who's going to inherit the house when he dies?"

"Nobody I know of. The town will probably burn the place down as there's things in them basements that shouldn't exist."

"Like what?"

"Like too many secrets. That's what."

The decrepit house was in serious disrepair. She followed Daisy across a patch of dead grass lifting dry dust with her feet. The sun was beating down on them making the air too heavy to breathe. Margo quickly looked around. There were no trees to provide shade, at least not here, in front of the house. Some dead shrubbery around the front stairs could have been ornamental bushes, but a very long time ago. The place's only redeeming quality was the visible stretch of pristine blue bayou twinkling far away under the boiling sun.

"So this John is the only caretaker here?"

"Yes. But he has a hard time keeping up. There's too much to do. He can only do the basics like keeping the cars clean and running, cutting the grass around the house and repairing something when it breaks. He also runs errands and gets groceries."

"That's still a lot. How about you, Daisy? What do you do?"

"I cook and do the laundry. I help Master Grott take baths, and shave, that sort of stuff."

"Who cleans? This house is enormous."

"We closed the upstairs down years ago. No point in keeping it up. John and I take turns mopping the floor in the living room, the kitchen, and Master Grott's room. I do his bathroom. It's a lot of work."

Daisy turned the knob on the warped, oversized wooden door and pushed with a grunt. Margo followed the woman and found herself in an unexpectedly beautiful room. Generations of merchants had owned the house and had filled it with all kinds of treasures from around the world. There were paintings on the walls in gilded frames and marble statues of exquisite beauty on carved wooden tables. Too much furniture competed for space with rugs and chests and more furniture.

"We don't lock the doors," Daisy said. "What would be the point? Nobody in their sane mind would come uninvited."

"But it's full of treasures."

"They're all terrified of Master Grott, I tell you."

"Who dusts all of this?" she asked, trying not to inhale too much of the humid, mildewy air.

"Nobody. We don't dust no more."

Feeling like an interloper in an empty museum in the middle of the night, Margo followed Daisy leaving footprints in the dust. The silence was sepulchral and absolute.

Daisy walked purposefully toward the main hall and stopped in front of the fireplace. She pointed silently at the painting hanging above it, and Margo looked. It was a life-size portrait in oils, magnificently done, framed in an elaborately carved, gold-leafed frame depicting a young blonde woman in her mid-twenties, richly dressed and coiffed. There were pearls around her neck and rings on every finger. It was a beautiful woman with clear blue eyes, very much the Nordic type. One of her shoulders had been painted bare as if the dress had slipped off her smooth white shoulder, and it depicted clearly a small black rose. It was under this painting that Josie and Billy had been photographed unsmiling some twenty years ago, the last time there had been a party in this house.

"Does she look like the woman on the beach?" she asked Margo.

"I'm afraid so. She's the spitting image of the woman on the beach."

"Please follow me. Master Grott would like to talk to you." Daisy looked away with a distressed frown, and Margo followed her to the next room.

Invited To The Big House

THE OLD MAN SAT IN A WHEELCHAIR by a set of large French windows overlooking a wild, unkempt swamp dotted by rotting cypress trees sitting in the brackish waterlogged land. Ducks were bobbing happily on the stagnant, murky water, oblivious to any alligators or snakes out there waiting in ambush to catch one of them.

The old man sat facing the window and didn't bother to turn around. His knees were covered by an old fashioned patchwork quilt with just the tip of his scuffed shoes showing, so she couldn't see whether he was as frail as they said, but his hands were crisscrossed with ugly purple veins and bruises. The silence in the room was asphyxiating.

When she told him hello, he finally turned the wheelchair and looked up at her. He was really old. Someone had said eighty years old. That was old, by her standards, and yet his eyes were clear, as the eyes of a much younger person. He still had hair and a lot of it, and it was beautifully cut and snow white. His face was lined but was still handsome in a jaded sort of way like he had lived too much. Somehow he didn't look like an invalid, but rather like someone who had just sat down in the wheelchair for a quick break.

"Miss Margo, I hear you've met our future guest," he said in a clear, well-spoken voice.

"I have indeed, sir."

"And what is your impression? Is she playing a farce?"

"I couldn't say. On the first impression, I thought she was lying, but it's uncanny how she knows things about the sloop, the people on it, and the cargo that she has no business knowing. Of course, I can't verify anything she told me because I don't have any internet—or a library for that matter—and therefore I have no resources to do research. But of course her story is preposterous. You don't come swimming ashore from a ship that went down over one hundred years ago. Besides, even assuming that such a supernatural event could occur, her heavy cotton gown would have made her sink. I saw myself how thick it was. You can't swim in one of those."

"Of course, of course. And yet, strange things happen every day in front of the noses of ordinary people, but they choose not to believe their own eyes because it's easier to deny than to think. Old Erma says that she saw the young woman walk out of the water. How could she have faked that?"

"It seems to me, Mr. Grott that you want to believe her story. Obviously, I can't tell you what to think, but science—if I remember correctly what I've read about these things—states that her story is impossible. Even if by some bizarre phenomenon she could have come back, her story is impossible to verify. And as to how she could have faked walking out of the sea in front of a witness, it can be done. Sometimes things seem impossible only until someone explains them. Like a magician's trick."

"Quite, quite." Striker Grott looked grumpy and irritated. "She's on the way here. I sent John to fetch her. I invited her to spend some time with us, recuperating. Maybe I'll find out whether she's telling the truth or not."

"And she said yes?" Margo shook her head, surprised. Did no alarm bells go on in the young woman's mind when she accepted such a suspicious invitation? "Why would she accept your invitation if you're a stranger to her? I wouldn't."

"John knows how to convince people. I'm sure she'll say yes."

"Well, I guess that's her business. At any rate, you'll find her to be an intriguing young woman. She's shy, and she has a pleasant personality. She sounds sincere too and appears to believe the story she tells, but I caution you. Don't get your hopes up. Not even in Louisiana can something like this happen."

Striker Grott stared into the horizon, pondering. Margo heard the ticking of the seconds in the imaginary grandfather clock in her mind. Then, the old man spoke. He had one last question.

"Does she really have the tattoo?

"Yes. The same exact tattoo. A black rose."

"I can hardly wait to meet her. Thank you for coming, Miss Margo."

The man turned his chair and faced the swamp again. He was back into deep thoughts and had already forgotten that Margo was still standing there, surprised at having been dismissed so rudely.

She followed Daisy silently back to the living room, and they stopped to take one last glance at the painting. The similarity was uncanny. She shrugged. No such thing as the supernatural, not this kind, anyway. Then they hopped in the car, and Daisy drove her back to the hotel. Neither of them said another word.

With almost an hour to kill before her meeting with Gloria, Margo went down to the beach followed by Pepper. She threw down a towel on the sand, and they sat there side by side and waited. Bonaparte Gulls rode the winds with long, synchronized movements, and Pepper twitched her little mouth and made soft noises as she watched them fly as if she was talking to herself. It was a seemingly idyllic town, and yet so many dark secrets lurked beneath its surface.

She struggled to remain interested in *The Moonstone*, but her mind kept going back to the dead body in the church, and to the mysterious castaway who was willing to go and follow a man she had never met to a remote house where an old man who could possibly be a murderer wanted to keep her close so he could find out if she was lying or not. No way was this going to end well. No way.

At times she looked up at the serene blue bay in front of her and watched the fishermen buzzing like bees around the shipwreck. Then she pretended to read some more. Every so often she looked at her watch and waited impatiently.

The Old Church, Again

PROMPTLY AT 1 pm., MARGO HURRIED DOWNSTAIRS and ran into Josie who was carrying a trayful of food for some late-lunch customers.

"Josie, glad to run into you. I had to close my door on Pepper because I don't want her to follow me to meet Gloria. She's safer here."

"Okay. I'll let her out after a while. You be careful out there." Josie looked fondly at Margo. "For some reason, I keep worrying about you."

"Don't worry. I'll be with an armed and capable policewoman who'll protect me. But we're just going up to the church to look at the books, and then we'll walk the trail to the other side of the hill. Nothing to worry about." Margo gave Josie a shy hug and then became bashful and looked down. "Sorry, you remind me of my mom."

"I never had children, sha," Josie said and touched Margo's arm gently, "but when I look at you, I wish I had. Now listen, we're having a council meeting tonight, so don't be surprised if you see the place full of old folks when you get back. But don't mention it to anyone. I'll explain later."

Margo nodded and told Josie a quick see you later. Suddenly she had remembered her mom and the ache that her passing had left behind. She had yet to figure out who had killed her and why, and not knowing had left in her heart a permanent sorrow that would not go away. But that was something she was going to have to confront later. Right now, she was heading for the police station because she had a mystery to solve.

When she got there, Gloria was in front of the station, exchanging a few quiet words with a young man in police uniform who introduced himself as Reggie Broussard, the only other policeman of Palmetto Bay. With a deep tan and a sun-bleached blond hair, he looked more like a

California surfer than a small-town policeman. After quick introductions, Gloria and Margo started off on the trail.

"I thought we were meeting by the water," Gloria said.

"Yes, well, I couldn't wait any longer."

They set off in companionable silence and followed the same trail Margo had the day before. The sun was shining bright and hot, and pretty soon Margo started sweating, but Gloria looked fresh and composed in her uniform. Once in a while, clouds sailed in front of the sun and provided a few minutes of shade, but they were too few and too far in between. The gentle breeze that flew in from the bay smelled fresh and salty but offered little relief against the heat and the mosquitos.

Gloria looked worried, and she was awfully quiet. She took long strides with her head down, and Margo almost had to jog after her. Margo thought about all the dead bodies she had come across in her short life, and how it didn't get any easier, but then Gloria had also seen many dead bodies during the war. Except that it was just not the same when it was your own loved one. Now Gloria was about to find out if the man she had loved so much had abandoned her without an explanation, or if he lay dead—murdered and forgotten—in the church. No wonder she was so quiet.

Gloria obviously knew the way like the back of her hand. When they got to the clearing, she headed straight to the side door. Margo was about to insert the key in the rusty lock when it yielded and opened to her touch with a metallic screech. She was absolutely sure that she had locked the door the night before. The two women looked at each other surprised, and Gloria put a finger to her lips and quietly unholstered her gun.

The beauty of the circular church had been ruined by the knowledge of the dead body upstairs. The decay and the neglect now seemed ominous. And now it was even worse. Someone had broken in last night. With heart pounding in her chest like flapping wings, Margo walked quietly as she followed Gloria along the side of the church, staying close to the wall, hiding behind columns and statues the best she could. Her legs shook as she tiptoed up the hidden winding stairs. She knew the stairs would squeak and there was nothing they could do about them. But she felt safe behind Gloria, and against her better judgment—the one that wanted her to run—she stayed and followed.

Up at the top of the stairs, Gloria lifted a hand in warning, and they stopped and listened intently for a while, hiding behind the last column. All Margo could hear was her heartbeats and the soft shallow breaths she was taking, but nothing more. Slowly she calmed down and wiped the trickling sweat off her face and neck. The church was empty and silent. They were alone.

Gloria ordered her to stay put and quickly vanished behind another column. She was back in a minute and pulled her into the loft. "We're safe," she said. "Whoever broke in earlier is gone."

Margo entered the room and gasped in shock. The place looked like it had been ransacked. Someone had opened every single box and drawer and spilled the contents on the floor. Books pulled off the shelves were scattered around the room, gutted, pages torn out. There were papers and clothes and photographs in frames everywhere.

Margo was a book lover, and to her, this was sacrilege. She ran from old book to old book, gathering them lovingly, putting them back haphazardly on the shelves. But Gloria told her to leave the books alone. They had bigger things to worry about.

"They even slashed the cushions and pulled out their stuffing. I wonder if they found what they were looking for." The two women stared at each other in horror.

"Someone followed me here," Margo said.

"Yes. Did you leave the door open?"

"No way. Of course not. I remember locking it up and testing it to make sure it was closed."

"Did you turn the key in?"

"No, I didn't. Josie told me to keep it until I left town."

"Someone else has a copy, then. The lock wasn't tampered with, but simply opened."

"Yes. And they were really looking for something. But why now? If they have a copy of the key, why did they wait until I got here?"

Gloria waved away her questions. She didn't seem to care. She looked haunted like there was only one thing on her mind. "Where is the body?" she asked, with a shaky voice. Her eyes were so sad that Margo wanted to cry. She was beginning to doubt that this had been such a good idea.

"There, in the office behind that wall. Are you sure you're up to it?"

"Yes, of course. The things I've seen in war, nothing can be as bad as that. Besides, I have to know."

Margo walked to the office stepping over strewn papers and porcelain shards, and sucked her breath in. Whoever had ransacked the loft had also done a number on the office. Papers, drawer contents, mail, anything you could think of, was scattered about carelessly. But nothing was as horrible as what they had done to the priest. Had she known this might be Gloria's friend, she would have never, ever, asked for her help. But it was too late. She turned around and lifted her hands to stop Gloria from entering the room, but the other woman was right behind her and saw it all. Like so much garbage, the body had been thrown unceremoniously on the floor.

Gloria shoved Margo to the side and ran to the body. She gently touched the rotting soutane and looked at the knife protruding from the chest. She touched the dead man's hair and the ring on his skeletal hand, and she talked to him softly as if she were comforting a baby. Margo truly didn't know what to do. She tried to get Gloria to stand up and leave the body be, but Gloria begged her to be left alone.

"It is him," Gloria told her. Tears had welled up in her eyes as she squatted next to the dead body and were now running down her face in a steady stream. She had opened the top buttons of the dead man's soutane and showed Margo the dog tags. "I thought that he had abandoned me, and yet he was here all this time." She put her head in her hands and cried.

Margo approached her and helped her get up. She hugged the woman and let her have a good cry. She too knew about the sorrows of losing a loved one and gave Gloria all the time she needed to pull herself together. Then, Gloria straightened herself out and wiped her eyes with her uniform sleeve.

"Margo, help me find out who did this."

"I don't know if we can. It's been a long time."

"Promise me that you will help me."

Margo sighed. What else could she do but promise? "Then we have to look for clues," she said. "I'll take this room and the living room, and you take the bedroom and the bathroom. Let's see if we can find something."

"I should do the office."

"No, Gloria. I'll do the office. Let me do it. You do the other rooms."

"Okay."

"Are you sure you're up to it?"

Gloria didn't answer. She just nodded and headed for the bathroom.

Margo walked back toward the office carefully avoiding the debris and the body. She was about to bend down to pick up a picture frame when she saw Pepper Paws staring up at her.

"What on earth are you doing here?" she hissed at the cat. "I thought I locked you in the room. You followed me, didn't you? You need to stay safely out of the way while I'm working." She grabbed the cat and placed her on the desk.

Keeping watch over the cat, she proceeded to examine the room systematically like her policemen friends had taught her back in Half Moon Bay. She had even devised her own tangerine wedge system that made you divide a room into sections, top to bottom, like taking wedges off a tangerine.

From time to time she looked in Pepper Paw's direction to make sure she was staying out of trouble. As she looked through things, she put aside books and journals that seemed to reference local life and legends. Letters from Gloria that the priest had kept, and phone bills, and other trivia, she gathered in a different pile. Those would be for the policewoman to sort through.

Then came the inevitable. So far she had tried hard not to look at the body lying in the middle of the room, avoiding it every time she turned, but she knew that eventually, she was going to have to take some pictures of him and check for clues. As she stared at the body contemplating running away instead, Pepper jumped off the desk and approached it. Margo shooed her away but she didn't budge. She was sniffing the dead man's hand where the ring was and then staring at Margo.

Remembering how Pepper had discovered the numbers written on the castaway's hand, Margo got down on her knees and examined the dead man's hand. All she could see was a tiny piece of yellowed paper, but the cat was looking at her so poignantly that she carefully pulled it out from in between the bones.

"It's just a piece of trash, Pepper," she said as she smoothed it out. But it was more than that. It was the corner of a letter, torn, with part of a postage stamp still attached to it. It could be a clue. So Margo got up from her squat and placed the scrap of paper in a little plastic baggie. But Pepper kept complaining and sniffing the hand.

"Oh shoot, Pepper, if you're trying to tell me that I should take his ring off, you're dreaming. I'm doing no such thing. And then again, maybe I should. For Gloria's sake, so she can have a keepsake to remember her priest by." Ugh. Once the thought had entered her mind, Margo knew her conscience wouldn't leave it alone, so she thought, might as well do it and get it over with. She approached the hand and braced herself. Nothing to be scared off, she kept telling herself. Just slip the ring off. It will be easy. Pretend it's a Halloween prop. There you go. All done. She finally allowed herself to breathe, now that she'd committed the horror of robbing the dead.

But the ice was broken, and it became easier to go through the dead man's pockets. But she didn't find anything else. They were all completely empty. She took some photographs for evidence, especially of the knife, and then stepped back. She had done everything in her power to help. The rest would be up to God, and to Gloria because she was getting out of town as soon as she could.

Then, as she was about to grab her backpack and leave the room, she bumped into the desk and banged her thigh on an open drawer. Annoyed, she tried to slam it closed, but it was stuck. It wouldn't go back into the slot. She decided not to care and almost walked away, but something made her turn back and bend down. She squatted and stuck her nose to the drawer to see what was keeping it from closing and noticed a package, a brown manila envelope. After some tug and pull, she managed to rescue it intact. It was fairly fat: oh, about an inch thick, or so, and it was addressed to Gloria. And to think that she had almost missed it.

It was time to end the search. Already the sun was heading down. They needed to finish this while they still had daylight to work with.

She looked around one last time and, satisfied that she had all the books and all the clues the place could offer, she gathered her finds in her backpack and went to look for Gloria. She found her in the bedroom, sitting on the bed, crying. She was holding a man's shirt to her face with her eyes closed.

"Come on, Gloria. We have to go. It's getting dark."

"I can't."

"I'm serious, Gloria. We have to get out of here. We don't even have a flashlight. Come on. I'll help you up."

"Is that a cat staring at me?"

"Umm, yes. It's Josie cat. Never mind her. Let's go."

Margo herded Pepper Paws and a recalcitrant Gloria—still holding onto her priest's shirt—out the side door and locked behind them. Not that there was much point in doing that. Someone out there had a copy of the keys already.

She wanted to talk about what she had found in the office but Gloria was too distressed. So she figured there was no point in insisting. There would be time to tell Gloria about the letter fragment, the ring, and the manila envelope later. She picked up the cat in her arms and headed for the trail.

The birds were chirping the last songs of the day. Gloria was still sniffling, but it seemed like the fresh air was doing her good. Hypnotized by the sound of the ebb and swoosh of the surf breaking on the shore and the rhythmic purring of the cat in her arms, she failed to notice other sounds around her. So it was a while before Margo realized something was rustling in the bushes.

"Gloria, did you hear that? There's something in the bushes."

"Huh?" asked Gloria, lost in her own thoughts.

"Gloria, listen. There's someone following us." Finally, Gloria snapped to attention and stopped. She closed her eyes and listened intently. "To my right, about ten feet. One person. We need to get out of here. This is not a good place to be ambushed."

They started walking faster with Gloria now in the lead. Margo was trying not to panic. She kept looking behind her shoulder, holding the cat in her arms, trying to figure out where the danger was coming from.

"Surely, if it was just one person in the bushes, he wouldn't try to attack two people with one of them being an armed policewoman?"

"And why not? He could have a gun. He might even be the one who killed the priest. Can't you walk any faster?"

"Well, the cat…"

"Just drop the cat. It got here alone; it can find its way back alone."

"I don't want her to come to any harm."

"Margo, don't you know your priorities?"

"Well, no. Sorry. I'm just a civilian, and I've never been chased by an invisible gunman among bushes before. Besides, my legs are so much shorter than yours. And these branches are scratching me, and my backpack is heavy."

"Okay, okay. Just put the kitty-kitty down and try to hurry up. It will be easier to defend ourselves if we get to the clearing."

Margo nodded obediently and put Pepper Paws down and shooed her away. Then, she made a bigger effort. She trotted as fast as she could.

Amazed, she watched as Gloria changed from a vulnerable, crying woman into a warrior, and she was awed. The older woman's eyes had transformed, and there was a new fierceness and an intensity to her that almost scared her. Gloria gathered the priest's shirt into a ball and shoved it into one of her pockets. Margo hustled on to keep up with her.

Having left the thickest part of the trail, they started jogging downward. Pepper Paws, sensing the danger, was right behind them. Margo's head was swimming with questions. Was this the guy that had killed the priest? Was he the one that had ransacked the church? And why was Gloria convinced this was a guy anyway? It could have been a woman, a strong woman.

"I can still hear him," Gloria yelled out. "He's following us closely. He's behind the bushes. But we're almost at the clearing and he won't have anywhere to hide. He'll have to make a move soon, or leave us alone."

He. Gloria kept saying *he.* If it was an unexpected attack, and the priest didn't see it coming, it could have been anyone, even a woman. Of course you had to have a very strong arm to penetrate the thick cloth of the soutane. And a very sharp knife. But what puzzled her the most was the why. Why would anyone want to kill a priest? Unless they knew his true identity and knew he was hiding something. That is if he was hiding something. And then, what could he have been hiding? And why?

Meantime, the women continued jogging, Margo working hard to keep up with Gloria's longer legs. Usually it was Margo who was in the better shape, better than anyone else she knew. But Gloria was unstoppable. She was a war machine. She flung the branches and the bushes aside as if they were made of cotton candy instead of scraping, dangerous, poisonous material.

Why did the priest have to die? Had the murderer found what he was looking for? Obviously not, or else he wouldn't be in pursuit. Maybe the answer was in her backpack. She mustn't lose it now. Maybe that was what the attacker was after. Maybe he suspected they had found something. Maybe he just wanted to make sure they hadn't.

For a split second Margo thought that if she didn't stop to catch her breath she would die, but Gloria noticed her slowing down and yanked her arm and pulled her as she went. She struggled on, jumping over twigs and rocks and sweeping aside the branches that slapped her as Gloria let them go.

"Is it much farther?" she asked with a raspy breath. "If I don't stop soon, I'm going to die."

"Not far," Gloria whispered back. "We're almost there".

Then the figure—who had somehow managed to get ahead of them—jumped out of the bushes with a knife. But by then Gloria was unstoppable. The adrenaline had accumulated in her body. Without even stopping for a heartbeat, Gloria kept going. She rammed the attacker with her shoulder, and as he staggered backward, shocked by the surprise attack, she punched him in the face so hard that he fell on his back. Then, in a move as swift and fluid as an angry wave, Gloria kicked the knife out of his hand. But she turned around to check on Margo, and in that one second of distraction the man jumped up and ran back into the bushes.

The two women stared at each other. They never had a chance to find out who their attacker was because of the balaclava that covered his face. But at least they were not hurt. Gloria was still pumped, hyperventilating, but slowly calming down. Margo had never seen anyone bring down a man with a knife quite like that before. All she could do was stare in awe at the other woman.

"Gloria, I can't believe you just did that," she said.

The Priest

GLORIA, STILL TRYING TO UNWIND, still in her own painful universe, headed up the incline toward the police station without saying much of anything. Margo watched her as she went, looking at the street ahead, never turning around. She wished there was something she could have done to console her. Poor Gloria. Understanding that she probably needed some alone time, Margo decided against following her. Besides, she was worried about Pepper Paws whom she hadn't seen again after the attack.

She walked around for a while calling Kitty, Kitty, but she didn't see Pepper anywhere. Margo swallowed hard, trying not to feel worried. Maybe it was taking her time to find her way back home. Or maybe she decided to enjoy the outdoors for a while and would come home when she got hungry.

She walked back to the hotel wondering what she would tell Josie if she couldn't find her cat. She pushed open the door to the Drunken Duck. A fairly large crowd was having an early dinner, and the smells of good, homemade southern food made Margo realize that she had missed lunch.

When Josie saw her sit down at an empty table, she came over with two platefuls of fried catfish and collard greens.

"I haven't had lunch either," she said and sat down.

"How do you know I haven't eaten?"

Josie laughed. "Because I run the only decent restaurant in town. Where else are you going to eat?"

"You're right, and I'm ravenous. This food is amazing. Your talents are being wasted in Palmetto Bay."

THE BLACK ROSE RETURNS

"Mais well, I'm stuck here forever," she said with a wistful smile. "How did your afternoon go?"

"I found a bunch of history books and journals up at the church, and I'll go through them later tonight. But I do have a couple of questions about the priest. Do you remember him?"

"Oui, oui, I do remember him well. I'm a Catholic, you know. I went to church every Sunday that there was Mass."

"What was he like?"

"He was younger than I am, handsome. And he was very kind and likable."

"But?" asked Margo, sensing hesitation.

"Well, he was a bit unconventional."

"How so?"

"Oh, I don't know. He had this way of walking that was too forceful as if he were uncomfortable in his soutane." Josie smiled to herself. "He fiddled with his clerical collar a lot. But you couldn't blame him for that, as hot as it gets around here. The church should invent a summer outfit for priests, poor things, having to run around in those long soutanes."

"You're right. I'm surprised nobody has taken that cause up yet. What else?"

"Well, he sometimes used vocabulary that was not appropriate coming from a priest. The first time we heard him use a four-letter word, old Erma almost fainted. But he was a charmer. Everyone liked him very much. I often wonder why he never came back." Margo nodded, encouraging Josie to keep talking.

"Then, there was the Mass. He didn't follow it very accurately. Sometimes he made the silliest mistakes. When you've been to Mass most every single Sunday of your life, you know it by heart. Then, his sermons were sometimes a bit scatterbrained. I don't know. He would ramble on for a while and get lost in his own story and finally say *Well, I guess that's Amen then.* That usually made the congregation giggle. But he was a nice man. There was something so vulnerable about him, you know? You couldn't help but like him. Sometimes I got the feeling that he needed a hug."

"Did he drive here every Sunday, or did he live here?"

"He didn't live in town, that's all I know. I assume he drove in, but we never asked, and he didn't say, I don't think. He wouldn't have had to drive through the town to get to the church because the road up the hill veers off the main roadway before the first house in Palmetto Bay."

"Did you know his name?"

"Oh, yes. Father Mike."

"No last name?"

"No. Just Father Mike."

"Was he close to anyone in town?"

"Mm, let me think. You know, I saw him talking to the postman a few times. Then there was young Freddy."

"Freddy?"

"Yes, that's the boy at the bait shop. Freddy Mouton. Young man, red hair and too many freckles. You can't miss him. He's the only one around here with red hair and freckles, except for his mom. He looks just like her. He's adorable." Josie laughed her throaty laugh.

"What about the postman?"

"What about him?"

"Have you known him long?"

"No, not really. You know, he's not from around here. I think he's from New Orleans. Why he would have wanted to move here is beyond me. But he's young as well. In his thirties. Nice enough fellow, I suppose. He comes in for beers a couple of times a week. And there he is. *Quand on parle du loup, on en voit la queue.*"

Margo turned around and she saw an attractive, confident young man in his thirties—as Josie had said—wearing a postman's summer uniform. Shorts. Yes, he looked pretty good in shorts. Healthy and tanned, like the sort of person who spends a lot of time outdoors, by the sea.

"Hey Benji," Josie called out to him. "Come and meet someone."

Benji approached the two women with a friendly grin. His tousled blond hair was sun-bleached, and his smile a sparkly white. He knew he was handsome. He approached Margo as if she were fresh kill and told her, moving in too closely, "Hello, gorgeous."

"Behave yourself, Benji. Meet Margo Fontaine, Private Detective."

As soon as Josie said that, his smile closed up like a trap, and he took a step back. Well, that was that. He became formal and businesslike. Margo hated that people always reacted that way when she told them what she did, even the ones who had nothing to hide.

"I hear you've met the woman who washed ashore," Benji said. "Is she doing all right?"

"She seems to be. She claims she comes from the sloop. Nuts, right?"

"Have the police talked to her yet?"

"I don't know. All I know is that Mr. Grott from the big house has invited her to convalesce there."

"Now, why would he do that?"

"Oh, I have no idea. I'm sure it has nothing to do with the fact that she looks very much like Mr. Grott's late mother, including that black rose tattoo she has on her shoulder."

"Have you met our police department?"

"Yes of course. Reggie Broussard and Gloria."

"Yes, Gloomy Gloria."

"Why do you call her Gloomy Gloria? She's a lovely person."

Benji laughed. "That's her nickname. And she deserves it. She's always serious. She doesn't want to be friends with anyone, and she never smiles. So, Gloomy Gloria."

"And she doesn't arrest anyone for calling her that?"

"On, no. I think deep down she likes it," Benji said with a vicious little smile, "because that means everyone leaves her alone. She doesn't like people very much."

The Missing Clue

MARGO WATCHED BENJI THE POSTMAN walk around the room and say hello to a few people. He came across as a nice enough guy, but Margo decided she didn't like him that much. Maybe it was those sharp incisors he didn't bother to hide when he smirked. She noticed that not everyone seemed to like him much either. She watched him work the room: slap people's backs familiarly, or flirt uninvited with the women. Some of the guests cringed. Benji was not as loved or as popular as he thought. That was for sure. Then, remembering Gloria's package, she turned to Josie.

"Do you by chance have a safe?"

"Well, yes, of course. We had one installed when we remodeled the hotel the last time."

"Would it be okay if I left something with you? Just until tomorrow?"

"Mais oui. Are those papers?"

"Yes. It's an envelope addressed to Gloria. I found it up at the church. She left before I could give it to her."

"That's interesting. Why would there be mail for Gloria up at the church? Wrong address?"

"No, Josie. I think it's personal." The bartender's eyes had narrowed into slits, and she looked at Margo suspiciously. She hesitated for a second and then asked, "May I see it?"

Margo took the manila envelope out of the backpack and gave it to Josie. She weighed it and turned it around and around, examining the handwriting. The envelope was sealed, but Josie checked that too. When she looked at Margo, there was a very small glint of hurt in her eyes. But it was there only for a second, and Margo thought she had probably imagined it.

She made sure Josie locked it in the safe properly. She couldn't be sure that the bartender wouldn't open it. After all, who hadn't read that steam from a boiling water kettle could loosen the glue on the paper? Josie was an avid reader. She would know. She could easily check the contents of the envelope and then glue the flap back on. Nobody would ever be the wiser. But why would she want to? Why would she care?

While Josie got ready for the night's famous *fais-do-do*, Margo strolled around looking discreetly for the cat. She walked down to the roundabout where Rodrigo Palma's stone statue surveyed silently the waters of Shark Bayou, and she inspected the bushes and the stone benches—placed at regular intervals—overlooking the now darkening deep blue water.

As usual, the area around the plaza was almost deserted. A couple of older women sat on a bench gossiping while they looked out to sea. One of them was eating an ice cream cone. They looked up at her as she passed by them, and they gave her an almost friendly smile.

Shadows were becoming longer as the sunset in its daily blaze of glory. Its last rays shone down peacefully at an angle, making the tips of the tight little waves sparkle like diamonds. Sandwich Terns flew in formation overhead and then dove one by one to catch their dinner. Out there to her left, the broken ship sat on the sandbank, waiting for its chance to slip back into the sea. Pirates must have thought this bay to be paradise. Deep enough to sail close to the beach, protected from the rough weather by the cliffs on both sides. And somewhere out there, a secret cove to hide their treasures in.

The roughly mile-long beach, with its lovely white sand, was scattered with palm trees and the remnants of kiosks that once upon a time—at the height of tourism—must have been filled with colorful beach goods, piles of fruits in vendors' kiosks, and lemonade and ice-cream stands. *Quel domage*. Now, they had been left to rot in the sun. Their canvas fabric remnants hung from the structures in decaying strips, exposing wooden and aluminum frames.

Margo kept calling Kitty, Kitty, looking behind everything and under everything, but there was no trace of the cat. She was getting more worried by the minute. Angry at the locals that they hadn't bothered to clean up the beach after the storm—thus making her progress along the dirty sand so much more difficult—she continued walking and stumbling, calling Pepper Paws.

Well, she had reached the end of the beach and had seen nary a cat, as they say. A natural formation of rocks that jutted out to sea had been improved upon and converted into a breakwater that reached out for about two, three hundred feet where it curved backward and ended up parallel to the shore. It blocked the waves and the surf providing calm waters for the little bay.

Hands on hips, she looked out to sea. This was the end of Palmetto Bay. Beyond the rocks were the open waters of Shark Bayou. To her right rose the low cliff on top of which Father Mike's church stood silently waiting for eternity. There was no cat anywhere. She felt defeated. She dreaded having to go back to the hotel and tell Josie that she lost her cat.

Since she had come this far, she figured she might as well climb to the top of the breakwater, to make sure the cat hadn't strayed this far, to make sure she wasn't on the other side. She could have fallen and hurt herself scampering down from the church. This far out, nobody would have heard her cry if she was in trouble.

The rocks were slimy and slippery but not so large that they would have been impossible to climb. It was much harder than struggling up a Climbing Wall, and she ended scraping her palms and knees. It wasn't until she was halfway up that she realized that there was a path she could have simply taken, and that made her feel like a fool. But once she made it to the top, where she joined the narrow walkway that continued out to the end of the breakwater, relief flooded her heart. There, almost at the end of the walkway, in the quickly spreading darkness, a creature that looked like a cat sat staring at her as if asking, are you coming, or not?

"Pepper, is that you, Pepper?" She ran happily to where the cat was sitting and picked her up. She couldn't remember the last time she had felt this much relief. "What are you doing out here, you naughty thing? Don't you know that I was worried sick about you? I've been looking for you all day." But Pepper jumped out of her arms and ran to the edge of the walkway and looked down beyond the rocks. Margo, determined not to leave the disobedient cat behind, followed her and bent down to pick her up again. It was then that she saw a tiny rowboat tied to an outcrop, barely visible in the penumbra below. It was tucked away behind the rocks, on the other side of the breakwater, completely out of sight of the town folks.

"And that's how she did it," she told Pepper with a satisfied grin. She picked the cat up in her arms and ran with her all the way home.

Books And Journals

AS ANNOYED AND AS COOPED UP as she had felt before, wondering every second of the day how much longer it would be before she could get out of Palmetto Bay, Margo suddenly realized that the desire to solve the numerous mysteries of the town had superseded her frustrations. Therefore, she hurried with great excitement toward the police department. She could hardly wait to tell Gloria about the boat.

The dusty streets were usually empty at all hours, doors, and windows closed against the Southern heat. But tonight—it was really night time already—there was a festive air in town. People were walking down the sloping street, heading for the Drunken Duck wearing their good clothes. Women walked with arms linked, and young mothers fussed at their children for not being obedient enough. People gossiped and giggled with anticipation. She even got some friendly hellos and cheerful smiles in passing.

The dogs in the front yards, frantic at the sudden onslaught of so many people, barked mindlessly without stopping, and those who were not restrained by ropes or chains, threw themselves angrily at the fences, looking like they wanted to bite someone. Palmetto Bay was as alive as a beehive.

Margo's exhilaration didn't last long, though. Gloria wasn't there. She had just missed her. She asked where Gloria went when she wasn't at work. Reggie Broussard, the only other policeman in town, had no idea. He had never thought to ask.

Margo was disappointed. Josie was busy, and Gloria was gone. And she had news she had nobody to share with. Ugh. She turned back toward the Drunken Duck. Even from far away, she could tell that Rodrigo Palma's plaza was full of people, old people, and young people, milling around. Outdoor lights had been strung up on the bushes and lower tree branches as if the fair was in town. Some people had drinks in their hands, and others were coming out of the Drunken Duck with paper plates loaded down with food. The jukebox was blaring *L'anse Aux Pailles,* and a few old-timers shuffled their feet to the Two-Step out there in a quiet corner. Children were stuffing their faces with cake.

Margo slipped into the hotel quietly. This party wasn't for her to attend, and she didn't want to intrude. At the top of the stairs, Pepper Paws waited patiently and hopped up on the bed as soon as she opened her door. Mais well, as Josie always said, she had to go through her morning's finds anyway.

She emptied the backpack and separated journals, papers, and books, into separate piles. There wasn't that much, only what she had managed to cram into the backpack. There was one large Bible, the really heavy one that had slowed her escape down so much, and she opened it to the front flap.

Many British and European countries began keeping birth and death records nationally in the 19th Century. Before then, it was up to churches to maintain registers of marriages, christenings, and burials. When colonial settlers moved to America, they brought these customs with them. Thus, churches were initially the sole keepers of vital records and the only places where it was possible to find information about an ancestor.

Written on the empty white flyleaves at the beginning of the old Bible, the records were detailed and extensive—although mostly in French—and included dates of marriages and baptisms and personal quotes. The writing was almost illegible, especially with the older entries. They used to write in that old fashioned, tight little handwriting.

She saw the last name Grott several times as she went through the pages, and toward the end of the records, the name Mark Driskoll, whom Jeanne the castaway had called her friend: the young man on board the Camilla Star. According to the records, he had married a local girl, had numerous kids, and had died of old age. How could Jeanne have known this? She spoke of him with such familiarity, as if she were really speaking of a friend. And the monkey. Where did she get the monkey story from? Why would someone make such a crazy story up? Why bother?

A knock on the door interrupted her thoughts and she put the Bible down. Josie, dressed in a flowery party dress, stepped into the room with a big smile. She had a small plate in her hand, covered by a napkin.

"Hello, sha. I saw you come in and I thought maybe you would like some cake. You should have stayed downstairs."

"Thank you, Josie, but I didn't want to intrude. I'm going through the books and papers I brought down from the church."

"Let me know if you find something interesting." Josie came into the room and put the cake on the night table. Then she sat on the bed next to Margo. She picked up Jack's photograph and turned to Margo. "Is this your young man?"

"He was once. His name was Jack."

"He's wearing a soldier's uniform, isn't he?"

"Yes. He was in the army."

"Was? Did he die?"

"Probably. He went missing in action. His uncle had a funeral for him, for closure, I suppose, but I never really could believe that he was gone forever."

"Maybe he's out there, somewhere, waiting to be found and rescued."

"Oh, Josie, I hope so. But so much time has gone by that I don't know anymore. There's this young Engineer I met during one of my cases, and we get along so well. He's the one I was going to go on holidays with when I got lost and ended up here."

"Pierre?"

"Yes. And I feel I'm being disloyal to Jack for enjoying Pierre's company so much."

"Mais sha, how can you blame yourself for having an *envie* for life? You're still so young. You can't expect your heart to shrivel up and stop feeling." Josie put an arm around Margo's shoulder and then got up.

"Mais well, make sure you come down and eat something. I cooked up a storm."

After Josie closed the door behind her, Margo went back to her finds, and she examined the journals. These were the personal diaries of the parish priests. One dated 1880 mentioned the Camilla Star, lost with all hands. The sloop had been heading for New Orleans when the storm struck. Many local boys and men worked on ships for extra money. One successful trip meant a year's worth of staying home with the family. After the storm broke, the journal mentioned that family members traveled to New Orleans hoping for the good news that never came. No bodies washed ashore, and no trace of the shipwreck was ever found, no flotsam, nothing. It seemed that the storm had swallowed the sloop whole as if it had never existed.

Another journal described a visit to Palmetto Bay in the early 1920s. One Joseph Standish was a guest at the house on the hill and mentioned with horror that the owner kept slaves.

"I followed him to the basement and was horrified to see a long tunnel under the house, barely illuminated by the wall torches that a young man was lighting ahead of us as we walked. The walls of the tunnel were made of wrought iron and were divided into tiny cells like cages in which human beings had been locked like animals. Some of them howled when they saw us and grunted with the same sound that dogs make. Others begged, or screamed, or yelled prayers in garbled French. They shook the cages, some with fury, but others with despair. Their eyes—milky white—looked like they had gone blind from being down there in the dark for so long.

"The owner walked ahead of me at a brisk pace, and I caught up with him and mentioned that slavery had been abolished. But he just laughed. It made the shivers run up my back. I wished so dearly to be somewhere else.

"'Why are they down here,' I asked, 'locked up like animals?'

"'Because that's what they are, my friend: animals.' He rattled the bars with his cane and some of the prisoners foamed at the mouth, getting spit on their dirty beards. I was horrified, but my host just laughed.

"'But why? Why down here?' I asked as I hobbled behind him.

"'I'm keeping them here until I need them,' he said. He looked at me, and I saw a hint of madness behind those dead cold eyes. 'I'll show you tomorrow,' he said. Oh how I wished to be far, far away.

"Next morning they awakened me very early. The sun was barely coming up. It had been a restless night, filled with nightmares of slaves, murdered, tortured, hanging dead on stakes, and other horrors. But what awaited me that day was worse than any nightmare I could have conjured up.

"A servant handed me a cup of hot brew and a chunk of black bread, and I followed the master of the house outside. Three horses stood pacing nervously, nostrils blowing steam into the wind, held by the same young man who had lighted our passage in the tunnel the day before. My heart was beating out of my chest. I had never ridden a horse, not formally anyway. I am a professor for heaven's sake. Besides, I had this horrible feeling that I should get out of there. I sorely regretted having accepted the invitation to the house on the hill and was hoping for an opportunity to catch a ride back into town. I confess that I was scared of my host. I looked around for a place to run to, but there was none. The servant guarded the back door with a stony face, and the land was a vast emptiness of everything except tall grass and brushes. There was just nowhere to run.

"'Come on, man,' the master told me. 'Let's get on with it. The slaves are excited. We don't want to make them wait.'

"He must have seen the panic in my eyes because he laughed again. It was a deep-throated, cruel laugh, devoid of mirth. 'It is fun. You will see.'

"So we all mounted, me with the help of the young man, and we waited. At a signal from the master, five men came running out of the tunnel. They were barefoot and bedraggled. They looked up at the sky disconcerted, and, blinded by the sudden brightness, did not know what to do.

"'You have five minutes, gentlemen. Start running. Go on. Run for your lives.' He cracked his whip on the ground for good measure, and the men started running. The master laughed maniacally.

"I will skip the worst of this story for I do not need to write it down to remember it as long as I shall live. Fact is we chased all the men down, one by one. The young man was allowed one kill, and he whipped the man he had personally caught until he bled. He cried for a very long time, the poor devil, but the young man never stopped whipping. Then he just whimpered, and finally he was still.

"Then the master turned to me. 'You are next. I caught this one especially for you,' he told me as he pointed to another poor bleeding soul slumped on the dirty grass. 'Go ahead, professor. Have a little fun.' But I could not take another man's life. I could not whip to death a man down. I could not hurt another fellow human. To my shame, I started crying and stepped back. I was terrified.

"'Never took you for a coward,' he said. But who was the coward, I asked myself? This was no hand-to-hand combat. He had a horse, a whip, and another man's help, and yet he called me the coward. He got down from his horse and picked one of the men.

"'Crawl, you imbecile,' he told the poor soul, taunting him, 'and maybe I will let you live.' And the poor miserable creature crawled as fast as he could while the master walked behind him and laughed his delirious cackle as he cracked the whip on the grass.

"I saw no way out of this nightmare but to escape. I should have stood up to them, but what could I have done? Outnumbered by insane men, without a weapon, I had no choice but to flee. Those men on the ground were as good as dead already. Nothing but a cavalry could have saved them.

"So—grateful that I hadn't dismounted, because I would have never been able to get back on that horse again without help—I rode back, barely knowing how I did it, but the horse, knowing the way, guided me to its home. I fell off the horse more than dismounted it and walked to the door shaking. The servant was still standing there with her arms across her chest. She had never moved. Behind that stony gaze I could sense the horror and the despair, but she could have not done anything for the slaves any more than I could have.

"'Hurry up and get your things,' she told me. 'I'll get Tom to take you to town.' I hugged her gratefully and began to cry. And I must be a coward because I never looked back. I rode back to town sitting in my place quietly, ashamed of my cowardice. And I have never really slept peacefully ever since either. I stared at evil in the face and I looked down and lost. May God have mercy on my worthless soul."

Mark Driskoll's Diary

MARGO SUPPRESSED HER URGE TO GAG. She put the journal down with revulsion and horror. The man on the hill must have been related to Striker Grott. The more she learned about him and his family, the more disgusted she became. Cruel, jaded, malevolent people, wielding the power that allowed them to get away with anything they wanted, without ever being made accountable for their actions.

She picked up another journal, and to her surprise, she realized that it had been Mark Driskoll's diary. He had inscribed the first page with an elegant and precise penmanship, with lots of added flourish to the M and the D that preceded his name. This was written back when people took great care and pride in their handwriting, at least those few individuals who knew how to read and write.

The journal was brittle with age. It had gotten wet at the edges, but for the most part, was quite legible. The leather cover was beginning to peel, and the M and the D that had been etched on its cover in gold foil had just about faded.

June 26, 1880

"Today I sail the Jamaican sloop Camilla Star from Martinique, from its major harbor Fort-de-France. The Captain, Perry Sands is an old buddy of mine and has been telling me for a long time how beautiful the bays and beaches of Louisiana are, so this time I have taken him up on the offer.

"As I look out on deck, I see the smoke being spewed out by Mount Pelée. I tried to climb the volcano more than once, attracted by stories about the beauty of its waterfalls and forests, but the climb is steep and strenuous, and I finally had to give up.

"I will miss Martinique and its stately homes and sugar plantations, and the beautiful Creole women that made my stay so pleasurable. But I have been here too long, and it is time for a new adventure.

"The rainy season has been held at bay by spectacular sunshine, and as I stand here on deck, I see in the transparent waters all kinds of colorful fish, milling about us with curiosity. And it makes me think that Mount Pelée is rumbling an awful lot of late and this might be the best time to leave.

"Finally the sails are full and the enthusiasm high as Perry Sands, my good friend, orders us on the way. The coastline is horrendously dangerous for navigation, but I am told that it is no challenge for our Jamaican sloop. Our sloop carries 70 men, including Perry Sands and myself, and 10 cannons which should protect us against skullduggery. And we even have a monkey on board. It is dressed in a funny circus outfit and wears a red fez on his fuzzy head. Not a friendly fellow, but he does screech a lot. It makes me wonder though, why would Perry Sands need to bring a monkey on board?

"I always make sure and check that my money belt, and my papers and documents, are safely hidden. I do not dare take them off even when I sleep. Some of the deckhands don't look very honest."

June 28, 1880

"The weather is holding. There is not much to do as the sails are happy and full, and the men lounge on the deck playing cards and drinking watered-down beer. The water smells atrocious in the barrels, and so the drinking of beer makes you forget what is going into your mouth.

"The monkey, which answers to the name of Maddock—G only knows why—refuses to be friends. It bares its teeth when I approach, so it is best to leave him alone.

"I have nothing to do either, so I fill my diary with drawings of monkeys, and fish, and the birds that fly overhead occasionally."

June 29, 1880

THE BLACK ROSE RETURNS

"Today I have been shocked to the bone. I am still shaking and can barely write. I had just left my cabin early in the morning and gone up to deck to enjoy some fresh air when I saw, from far away, a square-rigged brigantine as small as my hand in the distance. I had felt the ship turning earlier. Maybe that was what awakened me so early. It surprised me because I understood well the navigation charts that Perry Sands had shown me, and I thought that we were going to sail in a straight line for at least another day and a half.

"In no time the direction of the sloop was maneuvered around to head for the brigantine, and we were off after it like the devil was trying to catch up with us. Perry Sands stood on deck laughing like a madman, brandishing his sword in the air. I briefly thought that the world had been turned upside down on its head.

"Then, he ordered his men to fly the red Jolly Roger flag from the mainmast. The sailors whooped with joy and jumped up in the air. They ran back and forth, fetching their knives and swords. Some of the men took stations next to the 10 cannons on the top deck which I had naively thought were there to defend ourselves from pyrates. It was quite ironic that we had turned out to be the pyrates ourselves. They were small in size, probably no more than 4 or 6 pounders. But they would certainly help bring down a brigantine, especially if it was unarmed.

"I was dumbstruck, unable to understand how my good friend Perry Sands could be a pyrate. Then I looked up at the mainmast and the blood curdled in my heart. Who doesn't know that the red Jolly Roger flag means imminent death to all aboard and no show of mercy? These sailors were going to attack an unsuspecting ship and murder every single person aboard.

"With eyes full of the horror, I tried to approach Perry for an explanation. But the sailors would not let me. They pushed me to the side and ordered me to either get a weapon or get out of their way. Horrified, I stepped back.

"What followed was a blood bath. We overtook the unfortunate brigantine before it even had a chance at fleeing. Their ship was heavy with cargo, and we were as light as feathers. I realized at that moment why my friend had always insisted on manning a Jamaican sloop. It was because he needed a much faster, much more maneuverable ship.

"We got close enough that I could see the horror in the sailors' eyes. They knew it was pointless to beg for mercy. The red flag said it all. Fighting? That was pointless as well. Sailors, usually composed of luckless men either desperate to make a living, or kidnapped in the middle of the night in some God-forsaken port, have no motivation to fight. They lined up meekly to die, and the crew of my good friend Perry Sands, whose eyes were red and shiny with the excitement of the kill, ordered his men to cut off everyone's head. They were fast at least, and I have to give them that. And their swords were sharp, so the unfortunate victims on the brigantine didn't have to suffer for long. But for me, it was more adventure and more blood than I have ever cared to see. Knowing at this point that there was no reason for me to stand there and watch my friend gloat, I retired to my tiny cabin next to his and I prayed."

June 30, 1880
"The ship is quiet this morning. Drunken pyrates—because there is no use in calling them sailors any longer—lay around the deck, all 68 of them, drunk into unconsciousness. A terrible pounding attracted me to the cargo hold that is now locked. I heard begging and screaming coming from the belly of the sloop, and I tried to open it, thinking someone to be trapped by mistake. A big and angry padlock prevented me from opening the trapdoor and all I could tell those underneath my feet was *sorry*.

"I walked about and found not one person conscious. I got to thinking that my ship companions had not thought this attack through quite well. The food and water were down in the lower hold which seemed to be now full of people. They were the ones with plenty to eat and plenty to drink. The rest of us, topside, had nothing. I decided to consult about this with my friend, but his cabin door was locked, and I assumed he was too, drunk beyond reason.

"I had my own stash of hardtack and dried horse meat, and I brought that on deck and sat down on a neglected pile of rope and nets to eat it and wash it down with some stale beer. With everyone around me sleeping, and nobody to tend to the sloop, I felt somewhat uncomfortable. But the weather was still holding, and sooner or later the pyrates would wake up.

"It's midnight. Most of the sailors have scampered away, and the ship is silent. I took a stroll on the deck by the moonlight. The horrors perpetrated by the brutes on this ship have taken nothing away from the beauty of the night sky. Is it possible that Heaven cares nothing about the misfortune of others?

"Up there, the moon, as full and ripe as a swollen melon, shines its magical light on the dark seas, making the slow and quiet waves sparkle like gems, and on this humble voyager trapped in a moment of madness that he'll never forget.

"Down there, in the quiet, sleeping sea, mermaids and mermen may dream of unknown lands populated by the barbarians that sail their seas, and wonder what kind of God can create such monsters. I here, out here, all alone on the sleeping ship, I too ask God the same questions and pray to be released—as soon as possible—from the madness so that I can get on with my life and never have to look back on this, but pretend it was a dream that never happened. And maybe one day, I'll be able to forget."

The Council Meeting

MARGO STEPPED BACK FROM THE WINDOW. The party was going full steam under her window. This was what hope did for people. All it took was the promise that there would be money to rescue the town from certain death, and they joyfully threw themselves into the festivities. Mais well, good for them.

Margo felt reflective. She just couldn't read another depressing journal tonight if her life depended on it. After finishing the pineapple cake and licking the caramel sauce off the spoon, she threw herself on the bed next to Pepper to find comfort in the cat's company.

As she rubbed the soft, silky fur, she found herself thinking about the castaway. Had John, Striker Grott's caretaker, convinced her to go and convalesce at his house? She almost hoped not. The whole thing gave her the creeps. It baffled her that creepy old Striker Grott should even believe that Jeanne would accept. She would have to be nuts to do so, he being a stranger to her. Or did she know what she was getting herself into? It was obvious that the whole thing was a well-timed setup: the shipwreck, the castaway, the vintage nightgown, the black rose. And you had to wonder whether those numbers scribbled on her palm were a phone number. Was she going to call someone, an accomplice perhaps, someone who helped her set the whole thing in motion? Someone local?

Pepper got up from where she slept and stretched and then got closer to Margo to snuggle. Her mind rambled on. She was aware that people who didn't live with cats thought that it was nonsense to credit felines with extrasensory perception. Yet her own cats back in Half Moon Bay were amazingly intuitive and had found clues—clues that she herself had overlooked—that had been instrumental in solving cases.

Then here was Pepper. She had noticed the ink writing on the castaway's palm and found Gloria's broken rosary. And she had alerted her to the little boat resting on the other side of the breakwater. Had all these instances been coincidences? Could be. Perhaps cat owners felt such a feeling of oneness with their pets that they endowed them with extraordinary powers that the animals didn't really possess.

And yet, they did seem to have predictive powers and the ability to find things that were out of place, things that their owners were looking for, even if they didn't know what it was that they were looking for. And that was why cats made such good clue finders. Sadly, as long as animal science couldn't prove the extraordinary powers animals had, people would just continue refusing to believe in them.

Oh well, it seemed like this was as good a time to go downstairs and eat something as any—before the good stuff was gone. She closed the door on the cat and headed downstairs to the pub. The place was standing room only. It seemed to her that everyone had come in. All the doors and windows were open, and despite the cool breezeway, the air was hot and muggy and smelled of too much beer and body odor.

There, by the shiny bar, Josie was presiding over an excited crowd of people of all ages. She had stationed a wooden crate strategically and was now standing on it, bringing the meeting to order. She looked pretty in her flowery party dress. Her hair was up in the usual bun, and her cheeks were flushed with self-consciousness. Margo found it amazing how this one woman commanded so much respect from a town. She should run for Mayor or something. She remembered how on the first morning out there on the beach, people had listened to her opinion about the castaway with hushed tones and respectful attitudes. She was very proud of Josie.

Despite the frenzy, when Margo stepped into the room, everyone went silent and stared at her with some hostility, but Josie told them not to worry as she had sworn Margo to secrecy. Margo would never tell the authorities that they had found a treasure. She promised that to them. And so, the meeting continued.

Ravenous, Margo made a beeline for the buffet where an assortment of Josie's culinary masterpieces had been laid out next to bowls of fruits and pastries. The cake was all gone—quel domage—except for a few pieces of caramel pecans, but there were plenty of pralines and other delights she could eat. She filled her plate to the brim and grabbed a root beer, and headed to the mêlée. The crowd was restless.

"The point is," Josie was saying, "that if we turn the gold in, we might never see a penny of it. The government will find a law or an excuse not to give us a fair share. After all, our men have done the hard work. They put their lives at risk to bring out the gold."

"You know how it is when the news gets ahold of this. Someone will come forward and declare that they're the descendants of the original owners," a big burly guy said with an angry voice.

"Yes. And then it will get tied up in the courts for years, and meantime our town is dying, and the streets are breaking up, and the young people are leaving," someone else added.

"I say we keep it." The burly man said. That caused a huge show of hands and people trying to out-yell each other.

"Quiet, everyone," an old man by the jukebox yelled. He too had found something to stand on because he seemed unnaturally tall. He was almost screaming, trying to get people's attention. "Listen. We can't keep it, guys, it's against the law. We have to give it back to the rightful owners."

"Oh, shut up, Russ, and get back down here." A middle-aged woman standing next to him pulled him down from his box and he stumbled down. Probably his wife, Margo told herself with a smile. Women might not be in charge, but they sure knew how to rule.

"Okay everyone," Josie yelled, waving her arms above her head, trying to restore a semblance of order. People were getting really angry. It was obvious they were going to put up a fight if someone tried to take their treasure away. "Let's stop arguing. We all know we need this gold. We'll sell it, and we'll use the money to turn Palmetto Bay into the tourist destination it deserves to be. We've been arguing about this for two hours. But this is a democratic meeting, and we need to decide what to do with a show of hands."

"Excuse me, everyone." Margo put her plate down and addressed the gathering as loud as she could. "I might have some information about the gold." She walked to the middle of the crowd and gently pushed Josie off the crate, taking her place. Everyone became very quiet and listened. "I was doing some research just now, reading some old books, when I came across the diary of a Mark Driskoll and his experiences aboard the Camilla Star.

"Now as you all probably know, he was the only survivor of the shipwreck. He had kept a diary which he somehow managed to save when he made it to the shore. He wrote in great detail about the days he spent on board, and how the crew came about the gold." The people had quietened down and were listening carefully to Margo's words. They moved in closer to her.

"The Camilla Star was a pirate ship disguised as a merchant ship. It was a fast sailing Jamaican sloop with 68 sailors and one Captain aboard. On the third day after they left Martinique, the Captain ordered the red Jolly Roger flown—which as you all know means 'death to all'—and they attacked a peaceful merchant brigantine and killed everyone on board. They looted the ship and found the gold. Since Mark Driskoll never mentions the name of the other ship, we will never know who the original owners were. Whether you decide to keep the gold or to turn it over to the authorities, is your business. But at least you know that no legal heirs will be able to come and claim it."

Someone in the back of the room lifted his hand and was waving it with frenzy. "I have a question."

"Yes?"

"So do you think that it would be impossible to establish who the original owners were?"

"Well, mind you I'm not an expert. I should advise you to consult a lawyer, especially as we're talking about a lot of gold here. But it seems to me that if you don't know who it belonged to, morally—at least—the concept of finders, keepers should apply.

"You must consider that there is no comprehensive list of ships that sailed the seas between America and other countries. I'm sure that not even the experts can give you an idea, much less tell you what percentage of ships went down. Registers of merchant ships are extremely rare due to the original use for which they were created. They were not meant to be historical documents. They were simply annual records of the vessels that were in existence at that point in time, and once they were out of date or unneeded, they were discarded.

"As far as I know, no institution holds a complete set of American ship registers for the time when the Camilla Star went down. If Mark Driskoll hadn't made it to our shores and hadn't bothered to keep a journal, we wouldn't even know this much. I say, there is no human way to find out where the gold comes from. At least your conscience will be clean when you spend it."

"That decides it, then. We keep it." People went out of control. They got louder and louder, struggling to be heard above each other.

Finally, Billy walked over to Josie's side and whistled a couple of times. "Everybody, calm down," he told them. The crowd subdued.

"Eh bien, let's do this democratically. Show of hands if you think we should keep it, please," Josie continued. To the last person, everyone raised their hands. "We keep it then. Now the problem will be to sell it quietly and quickly."

"I might be able to help with that," Margo said. "I know someone who knows someone. So, hide the gold for now, and I'll let you know as soon as I can make a phone call or two."

Margo looked at Josie's radiant smile and wondered if she'd made a mistake. Maybe she shouldn't have offered to be the go-between in a deal that was not strictly kosher. But she had been carried away by the excitement of the moment and the desire to help, and there was no taking it back now. After all, it would be for the better good, right? To save a town? She pulled out her little black notebook from her back pocket where it usually lived, and she made a few notes.

"Whatever happened to that whiskey you promised, Josie?" someone asked. The concurrence hooted and cheered. Josie's husband

Billy wheeled out a tub full of seawater and pulled out a small barrel from it. Except for some rusting of the metal rings holding it together, it was for the most part intact.

"Why the water, Josie?" she asked.

"After years under water, the barrel would dehydrate and fall apart in no time. The boys are keeping the barrels in seawater until we have time to decant them."

"So you all are done with the salvaging?"

"Yes. There's more we could bring up, but Billy and the boys felt the sloop shift some more today, and they decided to let it go. It could slip right back into the water at any time. They've already pushed their luck as it is."

"Okay then, let's have a taste of that whiskey."

Day Four

Burying The Dead

MARGO OPENED HER EYES to the early morning sunlight. Awakening from a very pleasant dream, for a second she thought that she was back home. But then, despair flooded in. She was still trapped behind that fallen tree. How many more days before she could get out of Palmetto Bay?

She dragged herself downstairs making an effort to be cheerful and followed the smell of freshly brewed coffee. When the legendary goat herder Kaldi invented coffee in the 9th Century, he did humanity a great service. It was coffee's ability to power up the brain—even just by smelling it—that gave a big part of humanity the courage to get out of bed in the morning. She remembered Kaldi fondly. According to the legend, the Ethiopian goat herder discovered coffee when he noticed how excited his goats became after eating the beans from the coffee plant. It was a lovely story, whether apocryphal or not.

Margo found Josie singing softly to herself in the kitchen, listening to some Fifties music on the record player while she cooked. The head-turning smell of *Couche-Couche* on the stove made her salivate.

"Are you making fried cornmeal for breakfast?"

"Yes, Couche-Couche. Milk or cane syrup?"

"Oh, definitely cane syrup. I like mine good and sweet."

"Me too," said Josie with a good-natured chuckle as she brought the plates out to the table. "Where's your furry friend?"

"Still sleeping, the lazy thing. I'm going to miss her when I leave."

"We're all going to miss you, sha," Josie told her and patted her hand fondly. "It's a pretty day. I'm sure you're getting all cooped up, so maybe today would be a good day to get some sun. The beach is clean, and the water warm. Besides, what else is there to do around here?"

"Don't you want me to help you clean up after last night's party?"

"Mais non, sha. It's all done. Go get some sun."

Margo looked out the window. From where she was sitting, she could see a good stretch of the empty shore. The sea looked deep blue and shiny, and the white sands sparkled like mica in the sun. For a second—as she sipped on her café au lait—she imagined the same beach full of tourists, their colorful towels spread on the warm white sand while the children built sandcastles and chased large multicolored beach balls.

"Have we heard from the road clearing crew?"

"Oui, oui. I believe we have. The clearing begins today, they promised. It's okay to be happy, Margo, so you don't have to hide your smile. I'm happy for you that you get to go home soon."

Picking up a towel, a sandwich, and a bottle of water at the pub, Margo wistfully headed to the beach followed by Pepper Paws. There was no point in feeling so frustrated. Ugh. Why not try to enjoy the gorgeous weather for a while? Her vacation with Pierre had gone so wrong, but so what? There would be other opportunities.

She threw herself down on her towel, determined to have pleasant thoughts. As she lay under the gentle early morning sun enjoying the soft breeze, Margo remembered to be thankful for having such a good life, even if it sometimes came with inconveniences. At least—unlike Josie and the other people of Palmetto Bay—she got to go home to a pretty and vibrant town, and to a comfortable, prosperous lifestyle. It was ungrateful of her to complain so much.

With those thoughts in mind, she soon dozed off to the sound of the waves lapping the shore and the *gwit-gwit* cry of the hungry Sandwich Terns. Pepper—who she couldn't go anywhere without anymore—lay panting in the heat next to her. Cats!

It wasn't long before a shadow intersected itself between the sun and the girl, and Margo opened her eyes to see Gloria staring down at her. She sat up.

"Is everything all right, Gloria?" She asked. Gloria seemed distressed and nervous. "You disappeared yesterday without as much as a word. I was going to tell you that I found some letters and a package addressed to you. But you left so fast I didn't have a chance to give them to you."

"Yes, thanks. You can show me later. I hope you don't mind that I'm about to spoil your fun. Okay to sit?"

"Of course. Come sit on the towel with us or you'll get your uniform dirty."

"Thanks. How was the secret council meeting?"

Margo laughed. "It was anything but secret. The whole town was there. Why do you think it was supposed to be secret?"

"I think Josie initially had the idea of keeping the authorities and the younger folks out of it so the so-called elders of Palmetto Bay could decide what to do about the treasure. But nobody can keep a secret around here. I asked not to be invited. I asked her not to invite Reggie or Benji either. As a matter of fact, I told Reggie to work the night shift because I wasn't feeling well. That way I kept him out of Josie's way."

"How about the postman?"

"Yes, Benji. Funny thing. I haven't seen him around. Was he at the meeting?"

"Nope, didn't see him anywhere last night. But there were so many people. It would be hard to know for sure."

"I told Josie that if we didn't know about anything, we wouldn't be breaking the law by looking the other way. She's made sure to warn every single person in town about the importance of not mentioning this to Reggie, or to Benji"

"That's kind of sketchy."

"I know, but think about it. If they found gold or something, no, no, don't tell me. If they found something, the Coast Guard, the maritime lawyers, and the press, would all swoop down on this town without mercy. The notoriety might be good for all of a few weeks, but afterward, Palmetto Bay would be left behind, forgotten. And someone else would have walked away with the gold. So, who am I to tell what's right or what's wrong?"

"You're right. I find myself in the same dilemma. I offered my help to sell the gold. I know people who know people. And Josie was so excited. She loves this town. But I regretted my words the moment they left my mouth, but I couldn't take them back. I didn't have the heart. I kind of wish I hadn't said anything."

"Margo, I need help."

"Sure. What is it?"

"I've been thinking." Gloria picked up a handful of warm sand and let it slip through her fingers. Her eyes looked out at the bay, sad and forlorn. "I can't leave Mike out there in the church and forget about him. And I don't have the energy to do all this officially. It would involve forensics experts from out of town, and autopsies and investigations. Nobody is going to care if we go back up and quietly bury him somewhere. But you have to come with me and help me. I'm not brave enough to do it by myself."

"Of course I'll help. But I keep forgetting to tell you that the package addressed to you was in his desk, so it's probably from him. It might explain why he left. Should I go get it?"

"I'll pick all that up on the way back. Could you come with me now? Before I lose my courage? Will you hate me if I interrupt your beach time?"

Margo sighed with regret. She hopped into her shoes, shorts, and t-shirt, and headed with Gloria for the cliffs at the end of the shoreline, walking close to the water where the going was easier, leaving prints across the wet sand that were washed away by the waves as soon as they had been imprinted. Knowing the futility of arguing with Pepper, she let her follow them. As long as you don't get into trouble, she told her firmly.

They reached the bottom of the cliff and started climbing the narrow, semi-vertical path that led to the top where the circular church stood silent, abandoned, overlooking Shark Bayou and the houses of Palmetto Bay.

The further up they climbed, the more the distant horizon opened up. Margo stopped for a beat to catch her breath and to admire the clear blue spring sky and the pretty Sandwich Terns with their pale gray bodies, their short black crests, and their deeply forked tails, flying lazily overhead. The shimmering waters—hit by the mid-morning sun—sparkled cheerfully like the world didn't have a care, oblivious to the sorrow of the unhappy woman standing next to her, whose heart had been broken. And up there in the little church lay a murdered man—who had pretended to be a priest—who was after the treasure of bloodthirsty pirates who feared retribution neither from man nor from God, who might have found what he was looking for, and been killed for it. Yet all he had wanted was to live happily ever after with the girl he loved.

It was strenuous exercise—climbing under the Southern sun—and they reached the top of the cliff in a sweat, panting. But for Pepper, it had been nothing. She sat calmly next to Margo on a spot of grass and licked her face while Margo and Gloria caught their breath.

Margo grumbled. Gathering the decomposed body of a dead man and burying him in secret under this heat suddenly sounded like madness. But she looked at Gloria. She remembered Jack's last letter, full of hope to leave war behind and settle down to a quiet family life. Then, she remembered that other letter: Jack lost, missing in action. She knew them by heart, those two letters, and the loneliness of not having anyone to share your loss with. She couldn't let Gloria do this alone. She grabbed the policewoman's arm and gently steered her toward the church.

They entered the sanctuary, cool and dark in spite of the muggy weather outside, and headed toward the back of the church. The place seemed to have already aged so much even in the last few hours since she'd been there. As they walked down the nave, the multicolored light coming through the stained glass portraits of the Saints and the Blessed Family streamed down on her and filled her with sadness and a sense of loss.

"What's going to happen to the church? Do you think the town will try to restore it? Will someone at least rescue the organ and the artwork? So many beautiful things in here."

"Somewhere else, in some other town, perhaps. But here? Nobody cares. They're probably going to let nature take over, and in a few years, nobody will even remember that there was a church up here once. I hate to say this, Margo, but Palmetto Bay has become a cold, Godless place."

"What a shame."

"It is. The town is dying, the young people are leaving, and those left behind will soon die themselves and then, they too will be forgotten. Maybe it's time for me to go away as well. I have nothing left here worth staying for."

"I'm sorry about your friend."

"Yes, me too. He was too young to die. After all the sorties we survived together, after all the bombs that didn't fall on us, and the bullets that didn't hit us, to die murdered in a safe place like this, it's just too cruel. I thought we had a future together, and now I feel like I don't have anything left to live for. Life's not fair, Margo. No wonder people stop believing in God. Well, here we are."

They went straight to the office, stepping over the debris and the mess left behind by the intruder. The body was still there, where they had left it, even though Margo had secretly hoped that by some act of magic it would have vanished. They looked down at what was left of the priest—mostly just rotting cloth and skeletal bones—and she felt the old nausea coming back. She watched Gloria closely, worried about her. But the woman didn't even flinch. Her own feelings of dread, and the queasiness that came with it, well, she was just going to have to control them. Gloria was right in not wanting to leave her priest behind, and she couldn't let Gloria go through this alone.

"We have to carry him downstairs."

"I know," Margo whispered, bracing herself.

Gloria took a plastic sheet out of her backpack and handed Margo a white disposable face mask and a pair of surgical gloves. Matter-of-factly they picked up what was left of the desiccated dead man and placed him on the plastic sheet. Gloria looked heartbroken but never said a word, never shed a tear, as if she had lost all sense of perception. With efficient movements, she placed the knife in a plastic evidence bag and took Mike's dog tags off.

This was the end of a life. Regardless of religion or conviction, it was the ghastly truth. Flesh, and beauty, and awareness, ended up like this: nothing more than a sack of dried up bones. What was there to say? Gloria looked grim but determined, and all Margo could do was follow suit. When they were done, she picked up the nosy cat that had been sniffing at something in a corner and took the woven red twine bracelet out of her mouth before she choked. She gave her a hug a shooed her downstairs.

Once back down, they decided to bury Mike between the church and the sea, close to the bench, so that he could look out over the horizon for all eternity. The air was heavy with moisture and tasted salty in Margo's mouth. Birds and bugs seemed to have retreated from the unforgiving heat, and everything was silent around her. The Sandwich Terns were gone.

Gloria pulled out two collapsible shovels from her backpack and they proceeded to dig in a spot where the soil was sandy and relatively soft. They dug in silence, working under the heat of the sun, sweating, panting, and eventually Gloria—who probably had experience in this sort of stuff—stood up and said, "That should do".

Pepper Paws sat still to the side like a mourner at a funeral—as if she understood what was going on—as they lowered the body into the hole and covered it up. Gloria, with her voice cracked with suppressed emotion, read a poem Mike had written for her in another time, when they had both been happy.

And here under the clear blue sky, holding your hand,
Ignoring the voices and the ghosts from the past,
Just you and me and all eternity...

THE BLACK ROSE RETURNS

The poem was sad and wistful, and it presaged a future without a happy ending as if the dead man would have known that such a thing would be impossible. The last words of the poem floated on the wind: *"You are my life, and you are my salvation. I will love you forever"*, and Margo saw Gloria furtively wipe a tear away.

The sun was high above their heads when they arrived back to the main street. Gloria rejected an invitation to lunch but took the letters, the ring, and the package from Josie's safe. "Please stay," Margo asked her, reaching out for her arm, but Gloria just shook her head and left, heading back toward the beach. She never looked back. So Margo sat down all by herself to eat a gloomy lunch by the window that looked out to the sea. From there she could see the shipwreck that was now slowly slipping back into the water, flattening and collapsing on itself. The customers around her were too noisy, and the air-conditioner had been turned too high, and she shivered throughout her meal. Thoughts of ugly premonitions mingled with the bites of food. All in all, it was a terrible lunch. It wasn't until that moment that Margo realized that she had forgotten to show Gloria the little boat tucked away behind the breakwater.

The House On The Hill

MARGO WAS JUST ABOUT TO GET STARTED on her dessert when she saw Daisy—Striker Grott's frumpy Daisy—step into the pub and look around. She glanced at Josie with panic in her eyes, wondering if she still had time for a hasty retreat, but Josie just shrugged. She had been spotted, and short of being terribly rude, there was nothing to do but sit there and wait for Daisy, and whatever problem she had. Because, even from that far, Daisy's face said it all. Something terrible had happened in the house on the hill.

"Miss Margo, please, I have to talk to you," Daisy said and pulled out a chair without being invited to do so.

"Well, sure. Would you care for coffee, or for dessert?"

Daisy looked back at Margo and shook her head vehemently. There was definitely consternation in her eyes.

"What's wrong, Daisy?" she asked.

"Oh Miss, I don't know what to do."

"About what, Daisy?"

"John, the gardener, has vanished. And so has Jeanne, the guest from the shipwreck. And Master Grott is acting very funny."

"Are you sure? They might have gone for a drive. They might have gone for a walk…"

"No, no. Something's happened. I know it. Would you please come with me?"

"Wait, Daisy. Do you know something you're not telling me?"

Daisy looked at Margo hesitantly and then threw her head on her arms and sobbed.

"Come on, Daisy, you have to tell me. How can I help you if you don't tell me what's going on?"

"I warned Master Grott it wasn't such a good idea to bring her to the house. He's done something terrible, and now he's going to kill me."

"Nobody is going to kill you. What happened? I promise not to tell."

"I think Master Grott killed them. And he'll find out that I came to tell you, and then he's going to kill me too."

"Now, that has to be nonsense. Why would he do such a thing?"

"Well, it's like this. I've worked for Master Grott for many years. Before me, it was my mama, and before that, my Mamere. When I was a little girl, mama told me that the lady of the house had disappeared, and the chauffeur had disappeared at the same time. People said they ran away because Master Grott was too mean to them. But mama said she knew better. She always thought that Master Grott had killed them."

"But why?"

"Mama said he found them together in bed when he came back from a trip."

"I guess that's possible. What did the police say?"

"They didn't press charges. Master Grott has been in a wheelchair since he was young. They said he couldn't have done it."

"Well, there you go. He can't get out of his wheelchair to kill anyone. John and Jeanne will be back momentarily."

"No, they won't. I know they won't. I'm scared. If he finds out that I told you, he will kill me too."

"Okay, take me to the police."

They got into Daisy's beat-up Honda and went looking for Gloria. The young policeman was at the front desk. There was no sign of Gloria.

"Good morning, Reggie Broussard. We're looking for Gloria."

"I haven't seen her since yesterday. Can I help you?"

"I guess. Seeing as she's not here, you'll have to do. Reggie, Daisy has a big problem. John, the gardener up at Striker Grott's house has disappeared, and so has Jeanne, our castaway. Please hear her out."

By the time Daisy was done with her story, Reggie had fastened his holster on and picked up his belt and his patrol car keys.

"I knew it was just a matter of time before the old creep slipped," he said. "I've been watching him, but he knows it, and he has kept a low profile. He's old now, but he was a cruel, vindictive creep when he was young. He had the town terrified. There are stories and stories I could tell you about him. I wouldn't be one bit surprised if he'd offed those two. Hop in, girls."

While Reggie drove, he hammered out all his complaints against the man living up the hill; blackmail, contraband, murder for hire, trafficking of women and children.

"We've known for a long time, but we've never been able to nail him. He has a lot of money and all the lawyers he needs. And now a judge looks at him, sitting all pathetic in that wheelchair, and they say no way, this old man couldn't have done that. But that old man is a conniving snake. Why are you still working for him, Daisy?"

"Because I need the money, why do you think?"

They drove up the winding hill that overlooked the shipwreck and a patch of the clear, blue water. Reggie looked like he was boiling over with anger and resentment. Daisy sat in the back seat in the middle, frumpy, overweight, and uncomfortable in her tight clothes. All Margo could think about was that enormous tree log lying across the road between her and her freedom. This little town, brimming with dark secrets and resentments, was an outpost of hell. Reggie, Daisy, and the others, they kept insisting on embroiling her in problems she had nothing to do with when all she wanted to do was get out of there. She briefly considered climbing over or around the felled tree and walking to the highway, leaving her car and her stuff behind. She could always come back later for them.

"Okay, here we are," Reggie told her, interrupting her musings, and got out of the car. He patted the gun in its holster, and walked with big angry strides toward the house.

An ominous silence hung over the place. The air was hot and stagnant, with not a speck of breeze to relieve the heat. There was a stench of rot in the air, but it could just be the swamp behind the house. Margo reminded herself that she had a vivid imagination and that stench of rot didn't necessarily mean decomposing bodies.

She looked around for buzzards circling overhead anyway, or for any sign of life for that matter, but all that met her eyes was that dead heat.

They entered the house with Daisy lagging way behind. It was cooler indoors. Curtains had been closed to keep the sun out, and they stood in the foyer in the penumbra waiting for something, interlopers in someone else's house.

"Come on Daisy," Reggie finally said, breaking the silence. "You're the one who knows the layout of the house. Don't be a chicken." Margo poked Daisy to make her move, and finally she led them through the labyrinth of rooms to where the old man was gazing out at the swamp like he had the first time Margo had met him. Goodness, just the day before.

"What are you doing here, Reggie Broussard?" the old man cackled. "Have you found something new to accuse me of?"

"I will never stop accusing you, you miserable old man, and I'll continue hounding you until I have something on you. I want to send you to hell before you have a chance to die."

The old man laughed. "Sorry young man, but you wasted your trip up here again."

"We'll see. I'm going to look around."

"You need a warrant, don't you?"

"I'm going to look around anyway. Word is that John and your new guest have vanished. When was the last time you saw them?"

"Who cares when I saw them last. Go away." The old man turned his chair and went back to watching the swamp. They had been dismissed. Daisy showed them around the house, and between Reggie and Margo, they did their best to look around. But the old hound dog was clever—that is, if he was guilty. Because there was nothing to be found. The guest's room was also empty of clues, and Margo and Reggie looked at each other defeated.

"Why are we assuming that Striker Grott killed them? They could have left on their own," Margo said, wondering if they were overreacting.

"I'm telling you, Margo. This guy is guilty." Reggie was angry, and she wondered if Reggie had an ulterior reason for hating the old man so much.

"You could try John's apartment," Daisy said, and she pulled Reggie's shirt in that direction. "It's in the back behind the tool shed." Reggie shrugged and they headed outside. They walked the dry, scratchy path to the tool shed. The shed was impeccably organized. A small car sat in one corner, shiny clean as if it had been washed very recently.

"That's John's car. You see? He hasn't gone anywhere."

They followed Daisy to the back of the shed. She wiggled the door handle and made a comment about it being locked. Then, she stuck her pudgy hand in a small hole in the wall and poked out a key. She used it to open the door, and they entered. It was small but comfortable. It was also clean as a whistle, just like the shed. The bed was made. There was a computer on the desk and a great number of books on a makeshift bookcase. But there was no sign of John. "I have a bad feeling," Daisy repeated, wringing her hands. "I'm worried about John. I think something happened to him."

Margo and Reggie went through the place carefully.

"His clothes are all here," Gloria showed them when she opened the closet, "and look, this is his suitcase."

"How do you know these are all his clothes, Daisy?"

"Because I help him with the washing and the ironing. He's a nice young man. And that's the only suitcase he has."

"Okay then," Reggie said, sounding more than happy to believe the worst of old Grott. "You girls check the drawers and the shelves, and I'll see what I can find on his computer."

After a long quiet while, Margo exclaimed, "Holy Mother, guys, you won't believe what I found." Daisy and Reggie looked up startled. "Listen to this. *Mother dear, please let me come back home. I hate this place, and I miss you. I miss you so much. You know I can't live without you. My bed is cold and empty, and my nights are lonely. You promised me that if I was good, you would let me come back home. But now that Father doesn't travel anymore, I've been forced to stay away while he shares your bed and I pine for you. Why, why won't you let me come home?'"*

"Eww, gross. Did you guys hear that?"

Daisy and Reggie had approached Margo and were standing right next to her, reading over her shoulders.

"Here's another one. *'Mother, I swear, if you don't get rid of him, I will. It has been two years, and I'm still out here. You don't come visit me, you don't write to me anymore. Have you stopped loving me? Have you forgotten me?'"*

"Where did you find these?" Reggie took the letter out of her hands.

"Here, in this little box. There are dozens of them. They're all in the same handwriting, look. His mom kept them, and John must have found them. If someone had sent me letters like these, I would have burned them right away."

"He was obviously having an incestuous relationship with his mother. And look at the dates. The letters get more violent as time goes by."

"They disappeared one day, you know?" Reggie said

"Who, the parents? Yes, I heard."

"Nobody knows what happened to them. They just vanished."

"Just like his wife and the chauffeur," Daisy said. "At least that's what mama says."

"We're going to have to talk to your mama, Daisy if that's okay."

"Okay, let's get out of here. This place gives me the creeps." Reggie Broussard collected the computer and everything that went with it, and they headed for the car.

"You can't stay here any longer, Daisy," Reggie told her.

"I know. If I don't leave now, he will surely kill me."

They all walked urgently to the car, anxious to get out of there. The silence had become oppressive. The dry brush around the house rustled faintly when a small breeze swept by. But no birds chirped, no dogs barked. She wondered how Striker Grott would manage all alone in that enormous house—the invalid he was—with both Daisy and John gone.

"Did you bring the letters?" Reggie asked.

"Oh yes. I sure did. I also picked up a photo album. We can take a look at those at the pub. Oh, and there was a book titled *The Black Rose*. I have that too."

They sat in the car, each lost in their own thought. Then, Daisy said that she was going back home to her mother, and did Reggie and Margo want to come talk to mama. Reggie said he had to work on the computer, but Margo took her up on the offer. Reggie drove on and they fell silent again. Finally, Margo apologized.

"I'm sorry we made you lose your job, Daisy."

"It's not your fault. I'm the one that came got you. Master Grott's always been strange, but these last two days, he's been impossibly moody. I was getting scared of him."

"Well, I'm sorry anyway."

Before Margo got out of the car, she quietly handed Reggie a handful of envelopes written by a hand fond of curlicues and little hearts. "They're Daisy's. You better read them," she whispered in his ear.

Josie

MARGO STOOD IN FRONT OF THE Drunken Duck where Reggie had dropped her off and wondered what she was going to do next. Push the glass doors open and go find Josie, of course. But that was the last thing she wanted to do. As she stood there—indecisive, unmoving—she watched her exhaling breath turn to fog in the early cool air and realized she was actually very cold. She was shivering from shock. Watching Billy and Big Pete drive to their deaths had been a sobering experience. Suddenly, she was fatigued and forlorn.

She was struck by the deep silence around her. Besides the gurgling and swoosh of the incoming surf on the sand and the whispering of the breeze among the shrubbery, all she could hear was the beating of her heart in her temples. The town was still sleeping. How could so much have already happened while everyone dreamed on?

Down by the beach, beyond Rodrigo Palma's vigilant statue, the rare sight of a *bowl* of Roseate Spoonbills distracted her for a second. She watched them for a while, stalling for time, dreading to confront Josie. The pretty Spoonbills—easily recognizable even from far away by their pink bodies and bare, olive-green heads—were feeding as they waded in the shallow water, sweeping their bills rhythmically up and down, swallowing their prey. A multicolored beach ball—left behind the day before—bobbed on the water, back and forth, back and forth with the waves, dancing on the surf. It made her feel so sad, that forgotten ball. Suddenly, she wanted to cry.

She looked around, hoping to postpone the inevitable, but finally turned around and crossed the empty parking lot. She walked around the puddles as slowly as she could, pensively gathering her thoughts and thinking about how she was going to break the horrible news to Josie.

Her hands shook as she pushed the glass doors of the Drunken Duck. Josie had been so kind to her and how had she repaid her? By causing the death of her husband, that was how. And not only was her husband dead, but the treasure was gone. She swallowed hard.

The pub was as quiet as a mausoleum, the doors unlocked. Margo stepped into the silence and looked around. The place smelled of mildew, body odor, and stale spilled beer. The lights were off, but the circular neon sign that advertised the oysters was on, blinking as usual with a fizzy sound. Back in the corner, the colorful lights of the jukebox barely jumped out of the penumbra. But outside, the sun was beginning to come up, its light pouring in generously through the enormous windows showing the mess that had been left behind. Chairs were strewn about carelessly. Dirty plates and glasses had been piled up and left on the tables. For some reason Josie, who was so neat and clean, had neglected her beloved pub before going to bed. Her heart skipped a beat. Something must have happened last night. Up on the bar top, Pepper paced nervously, the hair on her back standing up, crying an anguished little meow. How had she gotten out of her room?

Josie, she called again and again, louder each time. When she got no answer, she looked around, wondering what to do next. Pepper jumped off the bar, looked straight into her eyes, and started walking to the back of the pub with her tail straight up in the air, the tip curled back like a question mark. Margo had never been back behind the public area and felt shy about intruding. But Pepper walked on confidently and she followed. She thought she heard a soft moaning coming from the silence, but she could have imagined it.

Pepper stopped at a door at the end of a narrow corridor and turned around to look at her, straight into her eyes. Uncanny how the cat could make herself understood. She stepped up to the door and tried the knob, feeling like an interloper. These were Josie and Billy's private quarters, where she had no business intruding.

She entered a large room that was almost completely in darkness. What meager illumination came in through the tall, narrow window, filtered through thick curtains giving her barely enough light to see where she was stepping. It was dank and humid in the room, and it smelled vaguely like blood. It raised the hair on her back.

Then she heard the whimpering. Disoriented, for a second she thought it was the cat crying, but then she noticed Pepper sitting by a prone figure lying on the floor at the foot of the bed. Her heart in her mouth, she quickly walked over to the crying figure, already knowing that it was Josie and that she was hurt, and wondered wildly if there was an ambulance in Palmetto Bay.

Josie lay on the floor sobbing softly. She took the few steps to the curtains and yanked them open. At that moment, she wished that Billy was alive so she could kill him all over again.

The room had been turned into a hurricane zone. Things had been hurled about with violence. The dresser mirror was broken. Vases, picture frames, broken. Closet doors were open and clothes hangers had been discarded. It was obvious that an angry and vengeful Billy had packed his stuff before he left. And there on the floor, at the foot of the bed lay Josie, beaten and bloodied.

She ran back to Josie and looked at her bruises.

"We need to get you to the infirmary," she told her. "You don't look too good."

"I'm okay, Margo. I really am. Just help me get up."

"Anything broken?"

"I don't think so. Right now, my heart is hurting more than my bruises."

"What happened?"

"Billy left me. He said he hadn't loved me for years, and he could hardly wait to get away."

"And he had to beat you one last time?"

"That was because I refused to give him back a small chest of jewels that he said he had salvaged just for me. I couldn't bear to part with it. It was after that other fight we had, when he begged me to forgive him. He looked into my eyes and said he loved me. And I believed him. That chest was special. I couldn't give it back."

"And he beat you for that?"

"Mais non, not only for that. I had also pushed a couple of the chests into the corner of the closet under some stuff because they were taking up too much space. Look at this room. It's so overcrowded with old furniture, there's no space for anything. But Billy insisted we keep all the chests in here anyway. He wanted them far away from prying eyes.

"But he was so angry and so hateful that I got nervous and couldn't think straight. Suddenly I couldn't remember where the other chests were. The uglier and more violent he got, the harder he hit me, the less I could remember. Finally he decided he had enough with the gold he already had anyway. He said he was in a hurry and, well, he took it out on me."

"Oh, Josie, I'm so sorry."

"It's okay. It's best that he's gone. He's always been mean and hateful. From time to time he got so violent that I wanted to run away, but in the end I couldn't do it. Father Mike tried to encourage me to leave him, but I never had the courage. I don't know if I loved him or was dependent on him, but I couldn't imagine life without him."

"So you think you'll be okay?"

"Oui, oui. I think so."

"You could always come to Half Moon Bay with me. You're a fabulous chef. We could open you a restaurant. Everyone would love you."

"Thank you, sha, but my home is here. There's enough gold to rebuild the town. I'll have enough to live a comfortable life. I like it here. My friends are here. My memories and the memories of my ancestors are here. You know how it is."

"I think I understand. Anyway, I'm glad you're okay," she said, cleaning Josie's face gently with a wet towel, "because we have to talk."

Daisy And Her Mom

THEY REACHED THE LAST HOUSE in one of the dead ends, and Margo followed Daisy to a cheerful-looking beach house. There were plants and flowers everywhere, filling the yard with color. A hammock, a dog, and a small bubbling fountain completed the picturesque setup. Margo followed Daisy in, and the girl yelled *mama*. The woman that came out of the kitchen was round and friendly, wore glasses, and had a mop of graying hair. She wiped the flour off her hands with the edge of her apron and then gestured for Margo to come on in. She looked surprised to see Daisy and asked, "Oh no, you haven't lost your job, have you?"

"How do you know, mama?"

"It was a matter of time. That's one crazy old man up there on the hill. I've told you many times to quit working for him, but you just won't listen. But do come in, Miss," she told Margo. "And who would you be?"

"This is Margo, mama. She's a private detective. The yardman and the guest from the shipwreck have vanished from the big house, and Margo is detecting their disappearance."

"Oh, you're the girl that's gotten stranded because of the storm. You're staying at Josie's, right?"

"Yes, that's me. Sorry to barge in on you like this, but Daisy told me you knew more stuff about Striker Grott than anyone else."

"Well, I did work for him most of my life. I never liked him—mind you—but he paid well, and I needed the job. He was not a nice man, but he never mistreated or disrespected me in any way. His obsession was elsewhere."

"What do you mean?"

"Daisy," she turned and told her daughter, "Go make us some lemonade, sha. Go."

Once Daisy was gone, she lowered her voice and told Margo in an ambiguous voice, "the old man used to sleep in his mother's bed, if you know what I mean."

"Did he truly do that? I thought it might have been all in his head. We found some bizarre letters in the guest house where the yardman was living."

"Ah, if John found the letters, he was probably blackmailing the old man, or trying to." Daisy's mom sat back in her chair with a pious miff. Her glasses kept slipping and she pushed them up the bridge of her nose.

"Was he that kind of person, you think?"

"John? Oh, yes. He was a crook. But a charming one, if you know what I mean." Margo saw with horror that Daisy's mom actually winked at her. "He always had a big friendly smile for the ladies."

"So you say Striker Grott had a thing for his mother?"

"Oh yes, it was an embarrassment. It seemed that his dead mother was everything to him. You would have expected him to have chased us, young girls, around the house, but he was never interested. All he ever did was stare at that painting on the fireplace." Daisy's mom sounded wistful as if she had found it disappointing that he had never chased after her.

"That was his mother Maude, the woman with the black rose tattoo on her shoulder, right?"

"Yes, Maude. My mama told me that the old man's father had bought her at a slave auction when she was but a *pischouette*."

"Striker Grott's father bought her like a slave when she was a young girl?"

"Oh yes. He used to sail to Martinique to buy slaves. He liked the young, pretty ones. This one came from a plantation called Black Rose something, I don't remember. Madame Grott told my mother that all the plantation's young girls were branded with that black rose on their shoulders. So the old Mr. Grott fell in love with young Maude and married her. He was a nasty old man, my mama used to say." Daisy's mom didn't even try to keep the lewd implications out of her voice. Margo suddenly had the urge to run and take a shower.

"Then one day, when the present Mr. Grott—Striker—was a young adult, the mother and the father vanished. My mama said she knew for a fact that he had killed his parents. He was mean as a child. Hurt the servants and the animals, so they sent him away to school. He kept begging to come home. After years and years, they finally let him come back, and that same summer the father vanished. And the present Mr. Grott took over. Come Christmas time, the mother had vanished too.

"There was another painting over the fireplace. The companion to the one that's there now. It was one of his father. He got rid of that one. He cut it up in pieces and then threw it into the fire. They say he hated his father because he shared his mother's bed.

"But that's not all. Two or three years later, he showed up with a new wife. She was a pretty little thing. Blond and blue-eyed like his mother. He made her get a tattoo on her shoulder that looked just like his mother's. It was so sickening. He was a mean, uncaring bastard to her until she relented and let him get her the tattoo, and then he changed. He became sweet and kind to her. It used to turn my mother's stomach, she would say.

"By the time I started working there, the wife was gone. Murdered, my mama used to say. Together with the chauffeur. It was the talk of the town, Miss. They used to say that he had come home from one of his trips to find the wife in bed with the help. And he blew their brains out and dumped their bodies in the swamp." Daisy's mom crossed her hands primly on her lap with a sanctimonious smirk.

"Is that what the servants used to say? Are you sure?"

"Absolutely. And that's what he did with his mother and father as well. That's what my mama said."

"Dumped them all in the swamp by the house?"

"Yes, the one that he's always staring at. He's probably wondering if one of them will crawl out of that swamp one day and drag him down to hell with them."

Daisy came into the room and set the lemonade tray down. The mother looked at Margo with a warning look and put a finger up to her lips.

"You know what's weird, mama? The woman from the shipwreck is the spitting image of the one in the painting."

"But how's that possible?"

"I have no idea. All I can tell you is that she has the same black rose tattoo on her shoulder and has the same honey-colored hair and the same eyes."

The three women stared at each other as they sipped on their lemonade.

Another Body

MARGO COUNTED THE HOURS as the afternoon dragged on. She could hear the ongoing buzzing sounds of chainsaws and wood chippers carried by the wind, which meant that the road would be clear soon, and she would be able to leave Palmetto Bay.

Pepper Paws was nowhere to be seen. She was probably scared of the pandemonium and was hiding somewhere. Josie was grumpy and busy and seemed to want to be left alone so, carrying a sandwich and an apple, Margo went outside and sat down on the bench by the beach, the really popular one where she and Gloria had sat when they had first met.

Funny how the shipwreck had already become a fixture on the horizon, but if you looked closely, you could tell it was slipping away. Up in the slowly darkening sky, the Sandwich Terns were flying away in formation, crying their gwit-gwit. Soon she would be leaving as well. She pulled the little black notebook out of her back pocket and leafed through her notes while she munched on the apple.

Whatever con John and Jeanne had tried on old Striker Grott must have backfired. She hated to think of the charming young castaway—who seemed so sincere and beguiling—as a con artist. The chances were good that Daisy was right and they had both been murdered. Otherwise, would they have disappeared and left the car and all their belongings behind? Unless the plan was to steal something from the big house and disappear by sea. There was the little row-boat behind the breakwater. Maybe she should check to see if it was still there.

Mais well, whether it was still there or it was gone, Gloria and Reggie were the ones who were going to have to unravel that mystery. They were not her business, these problems that haunted the inhabitants of Palmetto Bay, and it was not up to her to solve them as much as she found herself involved in them. She was just a reluctant participant in a drama that had been going on for generations.

In a way, she understood Striker Grott. He was a sick bastard for sure, but she understood. He was in love with his mother. It was the Oedipus complex: the son in love with the mother. It happened to all men when they were small, in some form or another: the desire to be mama's boy and the jealousy of the love that mother felt for father. Literature was full of examples: Oedipus Rex, Shakespeare's Hamlet, and so many others. Most boys outgrew it, but some got stuck in it. In Striker Grott, this childish desire turned into a deadly obsession, and he searched for and married the same type of woman as his mother Maude—with blue eyes and honey-colored hair. Then, with the addition of the tattoo, he turned his wife into his mother's spitting image. Okay, even that she understood. But where did young Jeanne come into the story? And what did it all have to do with the shipwreck? But even more disturbingly, why was Daisy lying? Because she couldn't get it out of her head that Daisy was, indeed, lying.

Margo took her shoes off and walked on the warm, wet sand toward the cliff. She might as well check on the little boat while there was still enough light.

As she walked the shoreline, she found herself thinking of Josie, whose bruises had just about faded, but whose sadness was not fading from her eyes. That Billy was an animal, trying to strangle her one day and asking for forgiveness the next. Margo was scared of Billy. She wondered how many times he had hurt his wife. Once she was gone, Josie's life would continue as if they had never met. She hated leaving her behind, but Josie was not her responsibility. It made her angry that she was going to leave two people behind that she had become very fond of, both of them living an unhappy and unfulfilling life.

As she got closer to the cliff, she sighted first the church tower and then the stone bench to its left, looking out to sea, almost invisible behind the bushes. It seemed like there was someone sitting up there. She squinted, trying to see who it was. When she recognized the color of Gloria's uniform, she picked up the pace.

"Gloria," she yelled and waved her arms, "what are you doing up there by yourself?" But there was no answer. So she yelled again and again. There was no motion coming from the woman sitting on the bench. It had to be Gloria, but Gloria wouldn't just sit there and not answer her.

Then, without any warning, a terrible feeling of premonition clutched cruelly at her heart, and she hurried to the foot of the cliff where the path began. With shaking hands, she climbed the escarpment as fast as she could, stopping over and over again to look up, to see if she could see the bench and its occupant better now. Her knees and hands were raw, and her heart was beating out of sync. There was something ominous about Gloria just sitting there and not moving regardless of how loud she yelled to her.

She climbed the last few feet in agony, sick to her heart at the thought of Gloria being hurt and ran to the bench, her whole body shaking. When she saw that there was a knife sticking out of her chest, she screamed in despair. Not Gloria, please not Gloria, she cried out loud, wishing she was having a nightmare she could wake up from. But it was no nightmare. She dried her teary eyes and looked at her friend. Already flies were buzzing about her open mouth from which a narrow strip of blood had trickled out and coagulated. Her empty eyes—now milky and cloudy in death—stared out to the sea. Margo's breath got caught in her chest. She wanted to shake her, poor Gloria, shake her awake.

"How could you," she screamed at the murderer. She looked around at the rustling bushes, her fists clenched with fury, thinking the murderer to be hiding among them. "How could you murder such a nice person? You're the one who attacked us, aren't you? You're the one who killed the priest. You coward. I'm going to figure out who you are, and I'm going to stop you. And I'll make sure you pay for what you did."

Anger made Margo snap out of the despair. It was going to be dark soon and she had to hurry. She looked for Gloria's backpack, the one she had put the letters and the manila envelope in, and she found it thrown to one side, in the dust. The letters were there, spilled on the ground, but the package was gone.

Margo got up and looked around. She listened intently. The rustling of the bushes in the otherwise silent early evening was unnerving. Far away she heard some children scream, and, a dog bark. But up there by the bench, she was all alone. The route through the bushes was too long and scary to undertake alone, so she decided to take her chances with the cliff. She clambered down looking over her shoulders, wondering if someone was going to try and follow her to assault her. What on earth was going on in Palmetto Bay?

She ran to the police station, not realizing that she was too tired to run and that she had lost her slip-on shoes somewhere on the way. By the time she got there, her feet were cut and burning, and she was beyond exhausted. She banged open the front door and entered—out of breath— her heart pounding out of control. Reggie sat at the front desk, the only desk in the office. He looked up from the computer at her, surprised by the noisy intrusion.

"Reggie, something horrible has happened," she told him. She felt like she was about to cry and was barely holding it together. Her whole body was shaking and she wished someone would just give her a hug.

"What, what?" He looked startled. He jumped up from the desk and took a couple of steps toward Margo.

"Gloria is dead."

"Gloria? Our Gloria?"

"Yes. Dead. Up by the church. There's a knife sticking out of her chest. You've got to do something."

"Like what? I have no idea what to do." Reggie's eyes had gotten as big as saucers. His breath came out ragged, in short strips, like he was about to have a panic attack.

"We need to get the people from the infirmary to bring her down."

"Okay." Reggie nodded vigorously.

"It's getting dark. It needs to be done soon."

"Okay." He nodded again.

"You won't be able to look for evidence in the dark, will you?"

"Okay," Reggie repeated, nodding rhythmically, staring at Margo as if he hadn't understood a word.

"Come on, Reggie. You have to snap out of it. I'll come with you."

"Okay." His eyes were now brimming with tears and his teeth were chattering. Margo grabbed his shaking hands.

"To the infirmary, Reggie. And don't you dare say okay again." This time, he just nodded.

While the nurses drove up to the church to bring Gloria's body down, Margo took the young man to the pub and had Josie give him something strong to drink. Josie brought a bottle of rum and three glasses. She sat down, shocked, but stayed quiet.

"What are we going to do, Margo?"

"Put Gloria in the morgue until the State Police can get here."

"We don't have a morgue," Josie said quietly.

"Then a refrigerator, or something. Whatever you have. Do we know when they will be done clearing the road?"

"They said tomorrow morning," Josie told her. "Phones are back. Internet is back."

"That's great. Okay, so leave Gloria in the refrigerator until the State Police get here. In the meantime, let's not forget that we have that other problem. Here, Reggie, have another drink." The young man swallowed the rum obediently and looked at Margo like an orphaned child.

"Tomorrow we have to look for John and Jeanne, remember? They are missing. And you need to check that computer that John left behind. You have to compose yourself, young man. We have a lot of work to do. We have to find out what's going on before anyone else gets killed."

Finally, having gotten himself together, Reggie left. But now all the sadness of what had happened in the last few days came together and Margo began to cry. Josie put an arm around her and comforted her.

Gloria, for all her tough exterior, had been a gentle soul. Margo really liked and admired her. She had hoped that they could remain friends. With all the traveling she did with her famous mother, she never really had many friends until she met Jack and went to college. Then Jenny was murdered and Jack vanished, and she fell into an emotional hollow, living life like an automaton, going through the motions. From the first day she had taken a liking to Gloria. They had only known each other for a handful of days, but Margo felt like she had lost a true friend.

Later that night, as she stared at the photo album she had brought over from John's room at the guest house, Margo realized two important things. One was that John had been planning this con for a very long time, and the other one was that John and Jeanne were twins. But that was not all. The greatest shock was the letter from Daisy, found tucked into the album as if it had been an afterthought. She wondered what Reggie was going to think about that.

Common sense said that it was way too late to go out. It had been an extremely long and stressful day. Margo was so exhausted that she could barely think. But Reggie had to see the photographs and help her make sense of it all. The pub was still full. Rumors were, the whiskey wasn't as satisfying to the modern palate as the town of Palmetto Bay had hoped, but it was obvious that they didn't care. They were drinking it anyway.

As she walked through the noisy pub, Billy was bringing out another barrel in the tub of seawater with the help of that big guy, the guy that had shoved her to the side when the fishermen got off their boats. He looked at her with his dead eyes and smirked. A loud cheer greeted the men, and many of the patrons hopped up and headed to help. Margo was more than happy to get out of there.

She walked with her hands in her pockets, carrying albums and letters in Gloria's backpack on her back. The night was cloudy and the stars and the full moon were nowhere to be seen. The street lights barely illuminated her gloomy thoughts as she tried to make sense of them. Twins. Who would have thought? But then, she had never met John. Otherwise she would have noticed how alike they were.

Most of the houses had gone dark, and her steps echoed on the empty pavement. A black cat chased another one in front of her path and made her wonder if she should believe in bad luck. A dog barked as she passed, and that woke up the other dogs, and they all serenaded the missing moon while Margo hurried on, hating to wake up the neighborhood.

The light was on in the police station, and she stuck her head in through the door. The bright indoor light almost blinded her. Reggie was sitting at his desk with big black circles under his eyes. The bright light made him look green and sallow. Margo figured she looked even worse.

"We have to talk, Reggie," she told the startled young policeman. "I found something."

"So did I. Come on in."

"Look at these photographs. I didn't know John, so I didn't notice the resemblance earlier. These are pictures that span two decades at least. He and Jeanne are twins. Look at this one. Mom and dad and two babies. Then, all these others where they are standing together, or playing together. Two little blondies, very much alike." Margo kept turning the pages, showing the boy and the girl turn into teenagers and finally young adults. "They had some con going with the old man."

"That's what I was about to show you," Reggie told her. "John didn't even bother hiding his files. I guess he figured the old man wasn't computer literate. These are emails he sent Jeanne. I mean, they start 'Dear Jeanne', so that's for sure. The interesting ones begin two years ago. I'm going to read you some excerpts.

"'Dear Jeanne, you won't believe what happened today. I'm in a place called Palmetto Bay. A couple of weeks ago, I started working for this guy who lives in a big fancy house up on a hill. Today, I brought some firewood into the house, and when I looked up, I saw this painting of a woman who's your spitting image. I couldn't believe it. Then, a thought occurred to me.'

"Then there's this one, a month later. 'Dear Jeanne, I've been thinking. If you did your hair like the woman in the painting, and you got a tattoo like hers, you could almost pass for her.'

"In this one, he's convincing her that it will work. 'Dear Jeanne, yes you will. Your eyes are the same color. Your hair is the same color. He's a confused old man. I think he'll fall for it. Just come on down to Cypremort Point and we'll talk plans. But don't come to Palmetto Bay. It's a very small town, and people will remember you. Better to give them the surprise. And don't forget to pack those old fashioned clothes. Nobody is going to believe you if you're wearing jeans and t-shirts.'"

"So where are John and Jeanne now?"

"I guess, if he found out what they were up to, Striker Grott could have killed them and dumped their bodies somewhere."

"Maybe he dumped them in the swamp where Daisy's mom says alligators ate them, or something."

"That would have been true a long time ago. Once upon a time the swamp was full of alligators, but they're gone. They were hunted to death. I haven't heard of an alligator around here in eight, ten years since I was a teenager. He would have had to take them somewhere far to get rid of their bodies."

"But he's an invalid, Reggie. How could he have done that? Although I must say he doesn't look too run down for an octogenarian."

"A what?"

"Oh, a man in his eighties. The problem is that he's in a wheelchair."

"But we only have his word for that."

"True. We'll have to go visit him tomorrow."

"I'm going to get Billy and some of his hunting buddies to come with us. John left all his clothes behind. Surely the dogs will be capable of following his scent."

"I have a bad feeling about this, Reggie."

"Yeah, me too."

Day Five

John And Jeanne

THE GROUP SET OUT FIRST THING in the morning. The air was cool, and Margo was grateful for her jacket. A brief storm had moved in overnight and had drenched the town leaving mud and mosquitoes everywhere. The dogs were excited. They thought they were going hunting. They milled about nervously, fogging up the air around their mouths and nostrils. Once in a while an excited yelp from one of them got them all riled up, and then Billy and the others would calm them down and order them to knock it off.

Finally, everyone was present, and off they went. Half of the dogs were in Billy's truck, the other half—give or take—went in the other one. Margo was perplexed at the overkill. They were all bringing their guns, rifles, and their Kevlar vests. Why did these men even have Kevlar vests? And were all these weapons necessary to find two missing people and bring down a dubious old man?

As the only woman in the group, she was voted down on everything she suggested, so she quietly hopped into Reggie's patrol car and stayed put. They arrived like the cavalry to the house on the hill which was as silent as death itself. With John AWOL and Daisy gone, it was probably just the old man in the big house, wheeling himself helplessly about, trying to survive.

They headed straight for the little guest house and Reggie fetched some clothes that they assumed belonged to the missing young man. And then the mayhem began. The dogs sniffed the clothes and went wild with excitement. They tried to out-bark and out-yelp each other, and at the first shout of *go*, they took off running.

Nobody had thought to keep them on a leash, and they left the two-legged crowd behind in no time. Margo just shrugged to herself. Hadn't she told them this would happen? Whatever. She got voted down on that as well, so now they could go run after their dogs like fools. She followed the men and said nothing.

When they saw the swamp water, the dogs went wild with excitement. One of them jumped in, and right away the rest followed. It was like a stampede. And then of course they had to be rescued because the edge of the swamp was so muddy that the dogs kept slipping and couldn't get out. So then, the men went after them. The Kevlar vests, rifles, guns, and ammo pulled them down with their weight, and they yelled out to shore that they were being sucked in by the mud. The whole thing was a mess. They had to be pulled out with ropes, wet as rabbits. All Margo could do was shake her head in amazement and wait for everyone to be rescued.

Finally, the hunting party got the gist of things, and they set out—wet, muddy, and grumpy for the humiliation they had just endured—in more of a regular formation.

They found the bodies after about an hour. It wasn't even nine o'clock. The two young people were side by side, dumped like trash, their identical blond hair blowing in the morning breeze. Margo had seen their photographs. She knew what they had looked like. But they didn't look like that anymore. They each had an angry reddish-brown bloodstain on their chests, where they had been shot without mercy. Granted that they had tried to pull one on Striker Grott, but nobody deserved to die and then be dumped like this.

The dogs lost control at the smell of blood and tried to tear the bodies apart. After a prolonged struggle, they were finally leashed and controlled. Reggie had brought a couple of body bags, masks, and gloves, and the men got busy. But Margo walked away. There was such sorrow in her heart to see that human beings were capable of doing this to other human beings. It was sometimes hard to have faith in humanity when you saw what they were capable of. Sleepy little town, my foot. It was more like a nest of vipers.

Once the bodies were packed and taken away, Reggie and Margo walked the perimeter of the dump scene, at least what remained of it after it had been trampled down so thoroughly by dogs and men. There were tire marks. Clear tire marks. The storm had left the soil so wet that not only the tire marks were well delineated, but Margo and Reggie could also see two very distinctive footprints walking side by side: one of a man and one of a woman. They looked at each other, surprised. The young people had either been forced to walk on their own to their dumping ground and then shot, or Striker Grott had followed them here with his vehicle and killed them when he surprised them.

"For a quiet little seaside town, there sure are a lot of murders around here," Margo told Reggie.

"It's not always like this, it really isn't. This is my first time investigating a murder."

"Well, we have to go back to the house and arrest the old man."

"But how are we going to do that? He's in a wheelchair."

"I'll show you how," Margo said, and stepped up her pace.

"He couldn't have done it. He can't walk."

"Reggie, I know he did it. And I'm going to prove it to you." And Margo refused to say no more.

The house was quiet. It already felt empty, musty. How do houses know that they have been abandoned? Their steps echoed on the marble floors as they went from room to room looking for the old man. They entered the great hall with the painting. Margo pulled Reggie over to the fireplace and pointed it out to him.

"Look at her, Reggie. Wasn't she a beautiful woman?"

"She sure was."

"Look at her tattoo. Did you ever meet Jeanne, the girl from the shipwreck?"

"Yes, I did."

"Doesn't this woman look exactly like she did?" Reggie nodded. "I think that John and Jeanne were going to make the old man think that she was the reincarnation of his dead wife. Except that they made a fatal mistake. The dates between the shipwreck and the arrival of the mother didn't quite match, but they were counting on Striker Grott's old age to not notice. It was a clever plan—and it might have worked—if Daisy hadn't told on them. How was she to know that they weren't making love in dark corners, but making plans for a better future?"

Reggie looked confused. It was obvious that he wasn't following. Margo shook her head. "Think about it, Reggie. Let's say Striker Grott is 80 years old. Let's say his mom was 20 when she gave birth to him. That would mean—roughly—that Maude, the mom, was born about 100 years ago. That puts her birth at around 1900 or 1910. Give or take. Right?"

"Yes, I suppose."

"The Camilla Star sunk in 1880. Maude Grott couldn't have been on that ship because she hadn't been born yet. She wouldn't be born for another 20 or 30 years. It's just too long ago."

"I don't know," Reggie said scratching his head, the math all lost on him.

"Anyway," she continued, "if she had been on that ship, she would have been like 40 or 50 years old when she gave birth to Striker Grott, in which case she would have been so old that he would have not been in love with her."

"But how could John and Jeanne know that the ship would come back?"

"Oh, they didn't. Nobody did. Until you're done going through John's computer, we won't know what their exact plans were. But when the ship surfaced, it was an opportunity. Jeanne must have been a clever girl. When she woke up in whatever place she was holed up in and saw the shipwreck out on the sandbank, she improvised. She grabbed the chance right away. She dressed in her vintage gown, waded into the shallow water, and waited for someone to show up on the beach. Then, all she had to do was "walk" out of the water, stumble as if exhausted, and throw herself on the sand. Then say a few intriguing words and let the people's imagination fill in the blanks."

"But Margo, you said she knew stuff."

"Yes, she did. That I haven't figured out yet, but they must have come across a book of local legends or some old journals. Maybe something John read up at the big house."

A screeching, metallic sound interrupted Margo and Reggie. They stopped talking and listened as it approached. In the empty, cavernous house, it sounded eerily haunting.

"Did you hear that?"

"Yes, I think it's the wheelchair."

They turned and faced the old man.

"It's you two again," he growled. "Why won't you leave me alone? Haven't you bothered me enough?"

"Striker Grott, we're here to arrest you for the murders of John—your gardener—and Jeanne, your houseguest."

The old man laughed raucously and looked at them with disdain. "You two are nuts. I'm an invalid. How could I possibly accomplish such a feat? Why, I can't even get out of my wheelchair."

"Yes, how?" asked Reggie, perplexed, looking at Margo for an answer.

"Well, I did tell you I could prove it to you, Reggie. Look at his shoes."

"Yes, what about them?" The young policeman turned to look at the old man's shoes, still not getting it."

"Look at them carefully, Reggie. They are scuffed, and there are traces of mud on them. How on earth would an invalid manage to get his shoes dirty, pray tell?"

Reggie stepped closer to the wheelchair and bent down to look, amazed at the old man's shoes. "They are really dirty. Mr. Grott, you killed your gardener and your guest. You're under arrest."

"I don't think so, sonny. I'm not going anywhere with you." He put his hands under the small quilt that covered his legs and pulled out a nasty-looking pistol. Then he hopped out of his wheelchair with the nimbleness of a man half his age. He walked to the fireplace waving the pistol and stood under the beautiful Maude's painting.

For a second, Margo wondered if this was the end, and they were both destined to die right there like reckless fools. But, no. Striker Grott just kept waving the pistol in the air melodramatically as he spoke. Margo had noticed before that—for some strange reason—murderers oftentimes feel compelled to confess their crimes and then to explain themselves. Striker Grott was no exception. He stood under the painting with a haughty, defensive attitude and told them why he had no choice but to do what he had done. Theodor Reik was right when he proved in his groundbreaking book *The Compulsion to Confess,* that because of unconscious guilt, criminals often leave clues that can lead to their identification and arrest.

"I liked John," the old man explained. "He was a good worker, and a nice young man. Believe it or not, I actually enjoyed his company. Then he brought this girl to the house. Boy, did she look just like my wife and my mother, black rose tattoo and all. I knew they were playing me. Their story was clever but full of holes. But it was amusing, and I had nothing better to do. I let them play along until I found out that they were fooling around behind my back, all over each other in dark corners around the house. That's where I decided to draw the line."

"Oh, Mr. Grott you must not have heard. John and Jeanne were siblings. They were twins. Did you not notice the resemblance?"

"You're lying, Miss Detective."

"No, Mr. Grott. I'm telling you the truth. They were trying to con you, yes, but they were not sleeping together. They were just enjoying each other's company as twins usually do. I'm afraid you killed them for nothing. And now you're going to prison for however long you may still live."

"I'm not going anywhere. I can't bear the thought of living in a tiny cell surrounded by idiots and criminals for the rest of my life. I would rather die. I've lived long enough anyway."

The old man lifted the pistol to his mouth, and Reggie stepped toward him, but he wasn't on time. There was a loud bang, and a sudden explosion filled the room and splattered Striker Grott's brains and blood all over the fireplace and the painting of his mother that he had loved so much.

Daisy

MARGO STORMED INTO DAISY'S MOM'S HOUSE, banging the front door open. Reggie Broussard, still in a fog of confusion—trying to figure out why they were there—was right behind her. Margo had refused to talk about it on the way down from the hill, telling him that she had things to think through.

"Daisy, I know you're in there. Come out, Daisy."

Daisy stepped out of the kitchen with an angry scowl on her face. "What do you want?" she asked.

"You knew all along that Striker Grott could walk, didn't you, Daisy?"

The girl shook her head and took a step back.

"You were his personal keeper. You washed his clothes. You cleaned his shoes. They got dirty sometimes, didn't they? You would have to be stupid not to understand what dirty shoes on the feet of an invalid mean."

"No, no, I swear I didn't know." Daisy took another step back, and she looked like she was about to run for the back door.

"He paid you well, Daisy. Actually, he paid you much more than a person in your position would normally get. Didn't he?"

"And how would you know that?"

"I've heard from several people that Striker Grott paid well. You've worked for him for a number of years. You kept his secret. He made sure you were satisfied with your salary, or else—squealer that you are—you would have told on him. Not even your mother knew.

"So tell me, Daisy, what did he pay you all that good money for? You might as well tell me now, because I'm going to find out anyway, and I'll make sure to find a reason for Officer Broussard here to send you to jail."

"All right. I did know." Daisy pursed her lips and looked resentful.

"Did you help him exercise? I noticed he was in amazing shape. Too good for an invalid. Did you help him, Daisy?"

Daisy's face was red with anger and embarrassment, but after a few seconds she shrugged and answered. "Yes I did. So what?"

"So he can walk normally?"

"Yes. He exercises every day. It took him a long time to get well after the accident, but he is like back to normal."

"Can he drive?"

"Yes. I've seen him."

"Did you know he was going to hurt John and Jeanne?"

Daisy turned away from Margo and lowered her head. She crossed her arms on her chest and refused to answer.

"Come on, Daisy. Out with it. The game's up. Striker Grott is dead. He shot himself earlier this morning. Did you or did you not know he was going to hurt John and Jeanne?"

"Oh, no. I didn't know."

"Then why did you warn me twice about the old man's behavior?"

"I never did that."

"Oh, yes you did. What happened, Daisy?"

"I don't know."

"Would you like me to tell you what I think?"

"No, Miss, please don't." Daisy looked down, defeated.

"Well, I'll tell you anyway. You're like what, thirty-five, thirty-eight years old, close to forty? Daisy looked away. You're getting old, Daisy. And you don't have a boyfriend, now do you? So this gorgeous young man comes to work for Mr. Grott, and he catches your fancy. How am I doing so far?"

"I don't know where you get this stuff."

"You told me yourself. You said he was a really nice guy. You did his laundry and his ironing. You obviously liked him enough to go to all that extra trouble. Plus, there are all those letters you sent him. We found a couple of them unopened in a drawer, another one in the trash can. Get your own conclusions."

"I'm not saying anything."

"But he's young and handsome, and he doesn't want anything to do with you. You hound him. You're getting desperate. You write him letters. You won't leave him alone. You've already dreamed up a fancy, imaginary life together with a pretty house, and children, and plants, and cats, and dogs. Every girl's dream: the house with the white picket fence. But he keeps turning you down. Time after time, he tells you he's not interested. I've seen the little love letters you sent him, so quit shaking your head. There's no point in denying it.

"Then suddenly, a pretty young woman enters the picture. She's everything you would like to be but are not. She's young, and slender, and graceful. Mr. Grott becomes enchanted with her the moment he meets her. You used to be the queen of the household, the one who ran everything in his life. Suddenly, you're pushed to the side. In a matter of hours you realize that your position in the household has been jeopardized.

"To top it all, John and the young woman are always whispering in dark corners, and giggling, and having fun. It drives you insane, doesn't it? How dare she come into your life and take your man away? How? So you quickly come up with a devious plan. You have to act fast before things get out of hand. You go and talk to Mr. Grott. Surely now, when he finds out that the girl is trouble, he will send her away. What was it that you said? 'I warned him'? After all, Mr. Grott fancies her for himself. He won't allow the help to take her away from him.

"But something went wrong. You didn't expect him to get up from that chair and go find them and shoot them, did you? That's why you came to talk to me. Because by then, they were already dead. Because you felt terrible about what had happened and didn't know how to tell me. You're a nice person after all, and you didn't mean for anyone to get hurt, did you?" Margo stared at Daisy until she obediently shook her head. "What happened then?"

"He said to help him throw them in the swamp. But I told him there are no more alligators in there to eat the bodies, and the police are going to find them in no time. So he said you're right Daisy. We have to take them far from here. I told him I didn't want to, Miss Margo. I really did. I begged him. But he pointed the gun at me, and he said he would shoot me too if I didn't help him do it. So I did. We dragged the bodies to the car and drove them to the woods. I wanted to bury them, but the old man was antsy. He wanted to get it over with. Just leave them bastards to rot, he said. That'll teach 'em to try and make a fool of me."

"Is that a confession, Daisy?" Reggie asked her. Daisy nodded. "Will you put all that in writing?" Daisy nodded again.

"I'm so sorry," she said. "I would do anything to take it back. I never thought that he would kill them. I just wanted him to send her away so I could have John to myself. I just wanted everything to be the way it was before she arrived. She ruined everything. I hated her, but I didn't want anyone to get hurt."

"You silly Daisy, you didn't even know they were not lovers. They were brother and sister, Daisy. They were twins."

"No," Daisy screamed, "no, no, it's not possible." Tears were streaming down her face like a waterfall. As Reggie led her to the car, she kept wailing. Reggie pushed her into the back seat of the patrol car, but it was as if Daisy hadn't even noticed. She seemed to have lost her sanity. The jealousy, the killings, the disposal of the bodies, and finally the guilt seemed to have pushed the young woman over the edge. Margo had the feeling that this was one person who would never be the same again.

The Storm

MARGO SAT AT HER FAVORITE TABLE in the pub, the one by the big window, eating a sandwich with one hand and doing research on the computer with the other. Josie came over with two cups of coffee and sat by her.

"I don't know if you've heard, but the tree cutting crew is almost done working on the tree. They should have the road cleared any minute now."

"That's great news, Josie. I don't want to sound ungrateful because you've been so nice to me, but I'll be happy to get back home. I miss my kitty cats—Ice and Fenway—and I miss my own life."

"Terrible thing about Daisy, isn't it? I always thought she was a nice woman."

"She does seem like a fairly nice woman, but she did something really, really stupid, Josie. By inciting the old man and filling his head with suspicion, she caused the death of two young people, and in the end, caused him to kill himself as well."

"Mais well, she's going to have to live with that forever. I'm not so sorry for Striker Grott, but I am for John and his sister. They were so young and had so much to live for, and what they did shouldn't have gotten them killed. Do you know what's going to happen to Daisy? Has Reggie said anything? I hear that her mom is devastated. Poor woman. Daisy is her only child."

"No, not really. I guess he will call the State Police to consult with them, and they will decide."

"Someone has to come for all of those dead bodies. We must be running out of space to hold them."

"So true. John and Jeanne, Gloria, and Striker Grott. Reggie is going to have his hands full clearing up all that mess." And as Margo's gaze turned toward the beach, she thought about Father Mike, whose body nobody knew about. Josie, too, was lost in thought.

"I don't know how you do it, sha," she finally said.

"What?

"Dealing with all those dead bodies and not going *motier foux*."

Margo looked at the little patch of garden vegetables to the back of the garden where Pepper Paws was sprawled, sleeping. She too sometimes wondered why murders and mysteries followed her wherever she went.

"That's why I try to find out what happened to them, you know? So their loved ones can find peace. And for myself. Whenever I see injustice or cruelty, I just can't seem to walk away. I rarely sleep well. I have too many ghosts behind my eyes, but I do what I have to do."

"How did you get started?"

"Oh, a few years ago a dear friend of mine from college was murdered by mistake. They were coming looking for me, and it was dark, and they didn't realize they struck down the wrong person. When she fell, she pulled the table cloth with her. Candles toppled, and the table cloth—which was old and dry—caught on fire. By the time I got there, the whole upstairs of the house was on fire. I tried to rescue my friend, but it was too late. Anyway, it's a long and sad story.

"But let's talk about something else. I've been doing some research. It appears that Gloria was all alone in the world except for her uncle here in Palmetto Bay. He'll get whatever Gloria left behind. And I can't find any relatives for John and Jeanne. I looked up all the names that appear in their photo album, but no luck. They don't seem to have any family left, at least none that I can find with my limited resources. Maybe Reggie will be luckier. And Striker Grott was the last of his line. He has no relatives left."

"*Dieu merci.* It was time for The Grott family's cruel bloodline to disappear."

"He was nice to Daisy."

"Oui, oui, I know. Maybe he was fond of her in his own way. He seemed to like John as well, and you tell me that he didn't hold it against him that he and Jeanne were playing games with him. At least not until Daisy started putting ideas in his head."

"Poor Daisy. She has three deaths on her conscience when all she wanted was to have a man of her own to love. Well, I guess if the road is cleared by tonight, I'll be leaving in the morning."

"Quel domage. We're going to miss you, Margo Fontaine. Palmetto Bay will never be the same without you."

"Thank you, Josie. I wish you were coming with me. You could open a restaurant in Half Moon Bay and have a more comfortable life. And I wouldn't have to worry about you." Margo looked at her coffee cup, embarrassed at her emotions. She didn't understand why Josie reminded her so much of her mom.

"Oh sha, it's so sweet of you to want to protect me, but you know I could never leave Billy. He wouldn't survive without me." Josie looked sad as if the light had gone off in her eyes. Whatever Josie's private torments were, she looked incapable of walking away from them.

"On another note, can you call a council meeting for tonight? I have news for you all."

"Can you tell me what it is, ahead of time?"

"What, and spoil my surprise?" Margo laughed and patted Josie's hand. "Not a chance. Say, Josie, is it me or is there another storm brewing?" At that moment, a large black cloud swept ominously in front of the sun and plunged the pub into semi-darkness. She looked out of the window and saw that the water seemed to be boiling in the bay. The ship out on the sandbank visibly shook under the onslaught of the angry waves.

The threat of a storm had come out of nowhere. Margo, noticing that it was going to start raining any minute, ran outside to rescue Pepper Paws. Already the temperature had fallen at least ten degrees, and a cold wind whistled up from the bay making her shiver. Thunder rumbled over her head, and every time lightning struck—out there beyond the bay— the water seemed to come alive like an explosion of fireworks. This storm was going to be a bad one, Margo thought, hoping dearly that the road crew was done picking up what was left of the downed tree on time, before all hell broke loose… again.

She ran inside with a perplexed Pepper in her arms and giggled when she saw Josie come out from the kitchen with a big towel. Just like a mom. She loved Josie.

"It's not raining yet," Margo told her with a grin. "But it's going to any minute."

The Argument

SUDDENLY, SOMEONE SCREAMED, and the thrumming of excited voices reached Margo and Josie, who were still drinking their coffee, chatting quietly by the window. When they looked up, they saw that a small crowd had gathered on the beach. It sounded like a brawl. Josie put her dish towel down and headed out. Margo was right behind her.

Benjamin Stoops—the postman—was standing at the end of the parking lot, right by where the sand began, having a heated argument with someone. He was waving his arms aggressively and pushing away another man, a much younger one, a red-headed, freckled teenager in a Hawaiian tropical shirt and cutoffs who was trying to hold on to him.

"You stay away from me, Freddy Mouton," the angry postman yelled. "I'm going with or without you."

"But you can't, Benji. The storm is back. Turn around and look. The ship is about to go under again. Look at the waves beating down on it. How long do you think before it sinks? You're going to get yourself killed."

"Leave me alone, Freddy. I'm going to go look for that gold. This is my last chance."

"But it's not worth your life, Benji. We'll look for another shipwreck. There are thousands around here. We just need more time."

"I don't have any more time. I'm tired of waiting." Benji zipped up his wet suit and grabbed a mesh bag with his stuff and the rest of his equipment. The small crowd had become a bigger crowd as the onlookers gathered around the two men. They milled around, but nobody made an effort to intervene.

Margo and Josie looked at each other. "Josie," she said. "You have to go tell him that Billy and his men found the gold already." Josie nodded, looking grim, and headed in the young man's direction.

"All right, Benji, I'll come with you. I can't let you go alone. It's too dangerous," the young man in the Hawaiian shirt was saying.

"Come on then, let's go." Benji started walking toward the pier, walking purposefully, dragging his equipment on the sand. Freddy followed slower, with his shoulders hanging. It was obvious he had no desire to go but felt obligated to accompany his friend. He had almost caught up with Benji at the pier when they heard yelling coming from afar, and everyone turned to see a red-headed woman in a summer dress and flip-flops running toward them. She was waving her arms above her head, screaming desperately.

"Stop Freddy, for Heaven's sake, stop. You can't go in. The storm is almost here."

"It's okay, ma. You know I'm a good swimmer, and I can take care of myself."

"Don't be stupid, Freddy. You're going to get killed," she begged. But Freddy bent down and gave his ma a kiss on the forehead and headed back toward the beach. "Hurry up," Margo heard the postman yell. "I'm not going to wait for you all day."

"Freddy, please. Don't go. You're all I have left. If something happens to you, I won't have a reason to live." Suddenly, there was doubt in Freddy's eyes, and Margo saw him stop. The postman was already walking dockside where his motorboat was tied. He turned around and yelled at Freddy with his hands around his mouth. The wind was picking up and getting louder. It was getting harder and harder to be heard above it. Josie and Margo tried to catch up with Benji, but the young man was too fast. Margo yelled, trying to stop him or to at least get him to turn around, but the wind was blowing in the wrong direction and swallowed her words and swept them away.

Meantime, Freddy had changed his mind. "Come on, man, let's think this through," he said running to the dock. He tried to grab Benji's arm, but Benji shook him off. "Ma is right," Freddy kept insisting. This is not worth our lives."

"I told you, Freddy. I'm going. With, or without you."

"Then at least give me my journals back."

"I'm doing no such thing."

"Give them to me, Benji. They belong to my family." So then, they started pulling on what seemed like a saddlebag, each trying to take it away from the other.

Finally, Margo and Josie caught up with the scuffling men. "Wait Benji," Josie told him, grabbing his arm. "What are you trying to do? There's no treasure left on the ship."

"Yes, there is," he spat back and shook Josie's hand off. "This was a pirate ship and the Captain's quarters were piled ceiling-high with chests full of gold and jewels."

"How do you know about that?"

"It's in the journals. In Freddy's journals. So someone has to go get it out before the ship sinks again."

"But we did find it, Benji. This is a suicide mission. Billy and the boys found it the second day they went out. You've been gone for days so you couldn't know about it. Margo is going to help us sell it, and we'll revive the town and bring back tourism. It will benefit everyone."

"That's a lie, Josie. You're just saying that to keep me from it."

"That's not true, Benji. I just don't want you to die. Haven't we had enough deaths?"

"What deaths? Nobody of importance has died. Mike was a dreamy fool, and Gloria was a stupid, whiny woman."

"What are you talking about? Gloria was a lovely person, and she was very fond of you."

"She was weak, and so was Mike."

"What Mike do you keep talking about, Benji?"

"Mike the priest, of course. The one you were sweet on. He was Gloria's lover." Margo inhaled quickly, startled by Benji's admission, and she looked over at Josie who had gone pale.

"Yes, Josie. I see you're surprised. He and Gloria used to do it up in the church attic. He wasn't even a real priest. He had y'all fooled, though, didn't he? Well, he had me fooled too. He was going to go treasure hunting with me, but last minute he pulled out. He said he was a loner, preferred to explore by himself. He had found some map in the church and he didn't want to share."

"So what did you do, Benji?" Margo stepped out from the crowd and confronted the postman. "Did you try to take it away from him? Did you fight? Was it you who stabbed him?" Benji didn't answer, but the truth was written all over his face. He took a step back toward his boat.

"Yes, it was you. You're the murderer I've been looking for." Margo suddenly remembered the red woven bracelet Pepper had been playing with up in the church. It was still in her pocket. She pulled it out. She grabbed Benji's wrist and looked at his other woven bracelets. "This is yours, Benji. It looks just like the others you have on your wrist. You lost this one when you were up at the church."

"He deserved to die."

"Why? Because he refused to give you the map? Seriously?"

"Well yes. Because we were partners. Because we were going to go treasure hunting together."

"And then, when he changed his mind and refused to share the map with you, you killed him."

"Yes, but it was an accident. We got into an argument, and I had a fish-gutting knife in my pocket and well, I hadn't planned on killing him, but I don't know what came over me. I had to show him that he couldn't push me away like that."

"Did you ever find the map?"

"No. I looked everywhere, but I never found it. After he died, I searched the church top to bottom, but I never found it."

"So why did you wait until now to ransack the church again? When I went up there the first time, everything was in perfect order."

"When I heard you were a private detective, I thought that Gloria had told you about the map, and you were up there helping her to search for it. I hoped that you had found it. I asked Gloria, but she said she didn't know what I was talking about. I accused her of lying. I knew she had it. But she didn't want to give it to me either." Benji's face betrayed the overwhelming desire that had been burning inside him. "I threatened her, but she laughed at me."

"So you killed her as well. For nothing, Benji, for nothing. She didn't have the map. Mike must have hidden it somewhere really, really well because Gloria and I searched everything in the church looking for clues to his murder, and we didn't find any maps of any kind. It must still be hidden there somewhere. You killed a lovely woman who was fond of you, for nothing."

Everyone gasped. Had the postman just confessed to killing Gloria and the priest? Through all this, Freddy Mouton was still yanking at the saddlebag and finally Benji gave in. "Here," he said spitefully. "Have your stupid books. I'm done answering questions. I'm out of here."

With long strides, Benji headed for his boat. Nobody tried to stop him. He threw his stuff in, climbed down the couple of rungs, hopped in his boat, and headed out for the shipwreck. He never looked back, and Margo had a horrible foreboding that this was not going to end well.

She looked around. Most of the gawkers were gone, headed back to minding their own business. A few fat raindrops fell, and the temperature dropped another couple of degrees. The wind-whipped sand slapped her and scratched her face and her neck. She wanted to go inside, but Josie was standing next to her, watching her with resentment, her arms across her chest. Margo realized belatedly that she had neglected to tell Josie about Mike and his murder, and about everything Gloria had told her. But then, it hadn't been her secret to share but Gloria's, and it was not Josie's business what Gloria felt anyway, yet Josie looked hurt and resentful.

Freddy Mouton and his mom stayed on the pier after the crowd dispersed, watching Benji head out to sea, his boat chucked from side to side by the angry sea. Freddy looked depressed, but his mom was triumphant. She held on to his arm possessively as she watched Benji head out to his doom. The sky was getting darker by the minute. The sea, that had been such a lovely shade of blue just hours ago, was now a dark green frothy monster and churned without rhythm as the waves slapped at each other. Benji's boat got smaller as it distanced itself from the onlookers. Tossed about like a child's toy boat, he kept steering steadily toward the decaying Camilla Star. Margo counted the seconds between lightning and thunder and realized that the storm was approaching fast, too fast. She grabbed Josie's resentful arm and pulled her toward the pub. She stopped by Freddy Mouton and his mom. She had a couple of questions that needed an answer.

"What was all that about?" she asked him. "What books were you talking about?"

Freddy bent down and took some books out of the saddlebag. "These books," he said, and he showed them to Margo. "This journal here belonged to my dad. This other journal belonged to my Papere. Benji wanted to read them so I lent them to him. They've been in my family forever. Ma would have killed me if I didn't get them back. These other books, Benji said he found them in the church."

Margo looked at the books and turned them around. "I have some stuff to tell you guys. Let's go sit down in the pub. I owe Josie an explanation."

Freddy Mouton and his red-headed mom followed Margo to the pub. The sky was rumbling, threatening to break apart. Josie was still angry, and Margo had to pull her along. Once everyone was seated, the adults with a beer and Freddy with a coke and a donut, Margo began talking.

"When I first got here, I was bored and frustrated, so Josie suggested I spend my leisure time looking into some old mysteries. I went up to the church upon the cliff and found a dead body dressed in a soutane, with a knife sticking out of his chest."

"Father Mike," they all said at one time looking at each other.

"Yes, it was your Father Mike. You can imagine my shock. I went looking for a policeman and I met Gloria, who came with me to the church to look at the body. But she recognized him and she started to cry. He was her secret boyfriend, and he was not really a priest. They had been in the army together and had a rough tour of war. When they came

back, Gloria applied for the job at the police station and talked Mike—
who suffered from PTSD—into impersonating a priest so that he could
move close to her. He eventually found solace in living alone, but close
to her, up in the church, where she could keep a protective eye on him."

"But he said Mass and took Confession, and all that. How did he do
it?"

"He learned from books how to. He was a smart man, and he did
well enough that nobody discovered his identity."

"So that's why he made so many mistakes," Josie said.

"Yes. He loved being close to Gloria, but he needed the solitude. A
church was the perfect place for him to find peace for his troubled soul.
That's why they never moved in together or got married. They loved
each other, but Mike needed to be alone. That poor woman you all called
Gloomy Gloria was just sad because Mike had vanished from her life.
She thought he had abandoned her without saying goodbye when the
truth was that he had been murdered." Freddy and his mom looked at
each other with embarrassment.

"Poor Gloria," Josie said.

"He was also an avid scuba diver and spent time looking for some
famous cove nearby where supposedly there is big pirate loot. Nobody
knew he was up there so he could come and go among the random tourist
without attracting attention. After all, nobody had seen him without his
priestly disguise. When you look at a priest, you rarely see what the man
wearing it looks like."

"Oh, the pirate cove. Yes," said Freddy, suddenly. "I remember.
Father Mike was actually good friends with Benji. Now that I think about
it, Benji went to New Orleans to get scuba gear about the time Father
Mike stopped coming. What, two years ago?"

"That's why Gloria couldn't find him. She went back a number of
times to look for Mike upstairs in his hiding place. But it seemed that he
was gone, leaving her behind."

"And when he did come back, he was murdered."

"When Gloria and I went back to bury the body, the place had been
ransacked. It was Benji. He was looking for something he didn't find—

now we know it was the map, obviously—because Gloria and I went through the place with a fine-toothed comb and there was no map. What I did find was a package with her name on it that had gotten stuck behind a desk drawer. That's why the killer missed it. It was in her backpack the last time I saw her, but when I found her up by the church, the backpack was empty and the package was gone."

"Is it this one?" Freddy asked. He picked up a manila envelope from the saddlebag. It was addressed to Gloria.

"Yes, that's the one. Benji stole it from her backpack when he murdered her. I had almost forgotten. Someone attacked us the first day when we were coming down from the church. I guess that was him as well. He was wearing a face mask, what they call a balaclava. I never saw his face."

"He was probably going for the backpack, to see if you had found something."

"It's hard to believe that Benji did all those horrible things," Freddie's mom said sadly. "And now to think that he might be dead too."

"What's in it?"

Freddy opened the envelope flap and took out something wrapped tight in cellophane wrap. "It's a bunch of money."

"Let me see,' Margo said. "They are about one-inch stacks. She flipped through them after she unwrapped them. "100 dollar bills. At about 250 bills in one inch, that makes it about 25,000 dollars in each pack. That's a lot of money. They're not new, either. I wonder where he got them. Anything else in that envelope?"

"Yes, a letter," Freddy said. It says:

'My dear Gloria,

'By the time you get this, I might already be dead. I'll be heading to the post office to send you this in the next few minutes. Since nobody knows about us, you'll be safe, but I'm afraid my days are numbered. I'm being stalked by someone who's just as devious as I am and must have military training as I do. And he's good. Because I keep trying to, but I can't catch him.

Agnes Makóczy

'There's a cove in Palmetto Bay, somewhere, where pirates congregated and hid their treasures. I couldn't find it, but maybe you will. Get yourself a boat with this money, and go look for it yourself, but don't let anyone get their hands on the map. It's very old. I found it here on the church shelves in a very old book.

'I made the mistake of befriending a local guy, the postman. He was bringing the mail, and I happened to be outside, sitting on the bench with my binoculars. When he told me he liked diving for treasure and was headed to New Orleans to buy some gear, I went with him. I knew what a mistake that was the moment I got in his car. He asked too many questions. I'm not used to dealing with people anymore, and under the pressure of trying to be friendly, I told him too much. But don't worry. I never breathed a word about you. You are safe.

'Take this money. It's not stolen. It's my pension and my savings. On second thought, go away. Go as far as you can and start a new life. But keep the map close to your heart. It's the only thing I can give you. And don't forget how much I love you.

'See you on the other side.

'Signed, Mike Logan.'"

"So where's the map?" Margo asked. "Was it here in the package all along?"

Freddy nodded and handed it to her. It was old and brittle, but it seemed so ordinary. And it was this that Gloria and her Mike had died for.

"You keep it, Freddy," Margo told him and handed it back. "Maybe one day when you're older, you'll decide to go treasure hunting. I'm sure Josie won't mind if you keep it, and nobody else knows about it."

Freddy walked over to the window and stared out to sea. The waves kept getting bigger and now they were seriously rocking the shipwreck. The postman's boat—tied to it—vulnerable as a toy, shook from side to side and at times vanished behind the waves. Benji was nowhere to be seen. Freddy stared at the shipwreck and would not take his eyes off it.

"He's going to get killed, ma."

"I know, son. But there's nothing you can do about it."

"I should have gone with him. He's my friend."

"You need to quit calling that *bon rien* your friend. He's a monster."

Freddy sighed. "But I shouldn't let him die."

"There's nothing you could have done, son. You tried to stop him. We all did. Besides, the sea is too rough. You wouldn't have made it back, and I would have lost you." Freddy nodded but kept looking out to sea.

Then the skies opened, and after a tremendous clap of thunder that shook the window panes and the whole building, it began to rain in earnest. Random people, who had been still lingering about in the drizzle, watching the shipwreck, ran from the sudden torrential downpour, banged open the doors to the Drunken Duck, and filed into the pub—soaking wet—with noisy enthusiasm. Freddy, loyal to the last, stayed by the window and stared out, even though all you could see anymore was the slate-colored outdoors where sky and waters had lost definition and had become one. There was no way to tell what was going on out there.

The rain stopped briefly in the early afternoon, and Margo went down to the dock with Freddy. The sun peeked out from the clouds tentatively, and a rainbow glimmered weakly at the edge of the horizon. Everything was soaking wet, and they plodded in the puddles of rainwater that were impossible to avoid. The tip of the tallest mast of the shipwreck was still visible, but it was going under, swallowed right in front of their eyes. And there was no sign of Benji or his boat. It was possible that Benji might have escaped, but what were the odds? It had been a brief but furious storm. More likely, Benjamin had drowned and his boat, tied to the rotting ship, had gone down, pulled along by it. But in the end, there was no way to know.

Margo put her arms on the young man's shoulder and led him back to the pub. "Come on, Freddy. It's over. There's nothing more we can do." The people were already gathering for the council meeting, but this time there was nothing secret about it. It didn't take the storm very long to come back.

The Last Meeting

JOSIE STEPPED ON HER WOODEN CRATE and vociferously made everyone quieten down. Excitement was in the air. People were milling in groups, laughing, chatting, and dreaming of a rich and fulfilling future. Children ran around with cupcakes and donuts, giggling and stepping on people's feet. It was a happy occasion, full of more hope than Palmetto Bay had seen in a very long time.

Meantime, Billy, Big Pete, and their buddies were all gathered back by the jukebox, drinking. Billy's face was dark and hostile as usual, and Big Pete's demeanor indicated that they had been arguing. The men, their buddies, were huddled in a group scowling. They were like a powder keg, those two, always sowing discord.

She recognized some of the locals that she had befriended: the nurse from the hospital, a couple of Josie's girlfriends, and old Erma, the one who had started the legend of the woman with the black rose tattoo who had come from the sea.

Freddy and his mom sat at the same table in the back by the window, Freddy still looking brokenhearted but his mom with a peaceful smile on her face. And then there was Daisy's mom as well, sitting with some women she had never seen before. She wondered why Daisy's mom had come, as unhappy as she should feel, and then realized how badly she must need some money to mount a legal defense for her daughter. After all the distress she had caused involuntarily with her arrival to Palmetto Bay, it made her feel good to have a chance to make up for it in a small way by helping to sell the treasure. It was the least she could do.

Josie had to scream to be heard above the storm that was now lashing the windows. Someone ought to have fastened the shutters, but hadn't, so now they banged against the windows, threatening to crack them.

"Guys," she yelled above the rumbling storm. "Margo has news about the gold. Everyone please take a seat and shut up. We need to let her talk."

"Thank you," Margo said as she pushed Josie off the crate with a giggle. Everyone laughed goodheartedly. Rumor had spread that Margo had good news. "I'm happy to announce that tonight there's nothing but good news. First of all, the drinks are on me." The crowd whooped. "It's a small way to thank you all for your hospitality and to make up for all the commotion I brought with me. Despite everything, I had a good time. This is a lovely town in a beautiful place, and it deserves to be saved."

The crowd was ecstatic. There was excitement twinkling in every eye, and hope in every heart.

"As I told you the other night," she spoke loudly to be heard above the storm, "I have a friend who has a friend. No names will be mentioned, but this friend has some suggestions. He told me to tell you that you can approach your problem in one of several ways.

"One, count all the gold coins and make an inventory. You'll find that they might have different types, like doubloons or reals or whatever. After you write up a careful inventory, have every witness sign it and put it in a very, very safe place. Take lots of pictures with your phones and cameras. Then turn the whole thing in to the state when they come knocking on your door—and they will—and hope that you get some or most of it back. At that point, whenever you're ready to sell part or all of it, he'll come and help you make the transaction, making sure you get the best possible deal. Remember that this is not just plain gold. It also has tremendous historic value. It might fetch a much higher price if sold to a collector.

"Two. The maritime laws for finders and keepers are many and varied and very complicated. Even if you do get to keep most, or only some of your treasure, the taxes will kill you. The friend of my friend has a more ethical solution if you prefer that one. Divide the treasure among the people present to spread around the tax liability. I've heard that that's what American Indians do with their casino gains. Everyone gets a piece of the pie. Say Joe will get ten gold pieces, and so will James. Already your taxes have fallen to a manageable size, especially considering individual deductibles and business expenses once you start renovating your stores. All that will be deductible. Cash in only as many gold pieces as you need for your living, or for your store, or whatever. Stay within your tax limit. If there's an accountant among you, he'll help you with that." Margo saw a pocket of excitement in the back and two hands were raised. They were accountants, she heard. She smiled.

"Three, and this is unfortunately what we have to do sometimes because as soon as the world finds out about your treasure, they are going to descend upon you and your little town like hungry vultures and will not leave you alone until you are bone dry. Keep the treasure a secret. Now you didn't hear it from me, but you'll be safer if nobody knows about it. I mean it.

"In any case, call this number without mentioning any details and ask this person to come visit. He'll know what it is about. He'll bring cash. He works for people who have a lot of cash. Let's say no more. Anyway, you need not worry that he'll cheat you out of a penny. Regardless of his other faults, he's a good businessman. It will be in his best interest to deal with you fairly. Should you feel that he's cheating you in any way, call me, or email me. I'll straighten him out. I know too many of his secrets. So I'm sure he'll play nice.

"I'm leaving on this counter a boxful of my business cards. They have my name, number, and email address on them. Everyone, take one please. And don't forget that tonight, drinks are on me. Salud!" She said and raised her glass to the others.

Margo got a standing ovation. She giggled as she got down from the wooden crate. How many people in real life get to find a pirate treasure? It was a lot more exciting than winning the lottery. Well, she was happy for them. If they were clever, they could leverage the gold to save their town and build a better future. Maybe their children would decide to stay home instead of leaving town as soon as they were old enough to do so. Destiny had given her—Margo—a second chance and had turned her life around. Now, these people could get their second chance too, unless they killed each other out of greed. But at least tonight, everyone was elated and playing nice with each other. You had to be thankful for that.

She walked over to Billy and Josie, who were doling out drinks faster than the speed of light, and said good night. There had been numerous dead bodies, but it had also been a good trip. It was good to see so many people smile.

She went upstairs to her room quietly, followed by Pepper Paws, her partner in adventures. She sat down at her computer and wrote Pierre a long email. How amazing. When the Camilla Star left dock one hundred and forty years earlier, the only way to keep in touch with loved ones was to write. Those letters sometimes took months, even years, to arrive, oftentimes getting to their destinations too late. But more often than not, they got lost at sea with the ships that went down, and then people would never get to hear of their loved ones again.

Dear Pierre, she wrote. I have quite a story for you. It was a long, convoluted letter mixed with stories about her trip to Palmetto Bay and regrets from the past. Then she turned her night light off and tried hard to fall asleep. The storm was sitting relentlessly above the hotel. Sheets of rain beat down on her window in waves, and gusts of winds whistled in through badly insulated panes. But by morning, the skies would probably be clear, and the sun would shine into her eyes and wake her up as it often did after brief, violent storms.

She remembered Benji heading stubbornly for the ship in the middle of the impending storm and wondered if he was still alive. She should have tried harder to stop him, and she debated her lack of action with discomfort. And yet—like her—nobody in the crowd had made much of an effort either.

Mais well, tomorrow morning, when she looked out of her window, there would be nothing left of the Camilla Star but the memory, washed away by clear blue, shimmering waters. She would have slipped back into the sea, this time probably forever. Then finally, hugging Pepper Paws who was purring up a storm, she dozed off.

Billy, Big Pete, And The Red Pickup

IT WAS ANOTHER TROUBLED NIGHT. While the storm raged on outside, Margo tossed and turned in her sleep. It was too hot and muggy. Fragments of dreams sent her walking on the sunny beach with Gloria, strolling barefoot on the warm sand with the surf playing between their toes. The Sandwich Terns sang their gwit-gwit and made little elongated shadows on the sand as they flew slowly overhead.

They were laughing at Pepper Paws who ran ahead of them and waded into the surf trying to catch some Orange Spotted Sunfish playing in the shallows, and Margo turned around to look at Gloria and tell her something. But suddenly, Gloria was dead now. She was lying on the sand with her milky white eyes facing the sun. There was a knife sticking out of her chest. And there were all those flies buzzing around her head.

Margo shook her head in despair and screamed. Someone standing behind her told her *please don't cry* and she turned around and saw that it was Mike—Gloria's soldier priest—trying to comfort her. Somehow she knew in dreams that it was him, even though she had never met him. He seemed so handsome and peaceful in his soutane. He opened his arms kindly and told her, *come let me comfort you,* but she kept crying. Gloria didn't deserve to die. Why did she have to die? She sobbed in her sleep. *There's no need to cry,* he said. *We're together now.* But when she looked up, Mike was gone, and it was Josie holding her. I wish I had never come to Palmetto Bay. *Don't say that, pauve ti bete,* Josie told her, patting her back gently. *Don't say that.* And Margo woke up with heartache and cried.

When she dozed off again—holding the warm, purring cat in her arms for comfort—she dreamed of Mr. Grott. He was a young man in her dreams, standing tall and proud under his mother's painting. The beautiful Maude smiled down at her son, exposing perfectly white teeth with sharp pointy incisors.

She looked at his shoes and saw that they were scuffed and muddy. She pointed them out to him but he mocked her and laughed at her with a black, toothless mouth. Cruel Striker Grott, you destroyed so many lives. *You killed your mother and your father,* she told him. *You killed John, and Jeanne, who were too young to die. How many more people have you killed, you monster?* Striker Grott thought this was funny, and he kept on laughing with a dry, cold mirth. *I'll never tell you, Margo Fontaine. I never will.* And then he grabbed his pistol out of a pocket and shot himself. Margo, reacting too slowly, extended her arms and stepped toward him to stop him, but he was dead already, his brains and his blood splattered on the painting of the beautiful Maude—his smiling mother—behind him.

A big clap of thunder shook the window, and Margo sat up, startled, wide awake. Her neck was sweaty and her moist pajama top stuck to her feverish skin. Pepper was sitting on the window sill, looking down at the parking lot, staring mesmerized at something. Her little mouth moved as if she was chattering.

There were voices under her window. Two people were arguing loudly. She recognized their voices even before she got to the window. Without turning her lights on, she carefully peeked out, making sure she couldn't be seen. It wasn't raining anymore and she could see the two bickering men clearly by the illumination coming from the hotel Welcome neon sign. It was Billy and Big Pete, drunk, and at it again, shoving each other around and hurling insults. She hated to say this, but Josie was a fool to believe that her awful husband had reformed. There he was, drinking again.

She watched them for a while, trying to listen to what they were saying. Then Billy went inside, and Big Pete leaned against a beat-up red pickup truck and lighted a cigarette. Margo was fascinated by Big Pete—like she would be fascinated by a cobra or a jackal—by his hostility and by his strength. It was like staring at evil and being unable to look away.

She watched the smoke rise from his cigarette as it slowly curled away covering his face in a haze.

She was about to grab Pepper and return to bed when Billy came back out. He was dragging a large wooden chest behind him, grunting and cursing with the effort. He growled something that sounded like help me, and Big Pete tossed his cigarette to the ground with a flick of his finger and joined Billy. They carried the chest to the beat-up red pickup truck that Big Pete had been leaning against. Then, they both vanished from her view.

Margo waited, wondering what was going on. They must have gone inside together. The minutes ticked by and she thought, well that's it, when she saw the two men come out with another chest. This was all wrong. They must be the ones the men had brought from the shipwreck. These were the treasure chests. At least she was pretty sure, she told herself.

The horror of what was going on invaded her and she hesitated. She was very scared of Billy and of Big Pete, and she really didn't want to get involved in anything concerning them, but if these two were stealing the gold, she had to warn someone. Not Josie. Josie would be unable to stop them. Billy would hit her again and make her shut up. And nobody in their sane mind would stand up to Big Pete.

Pepper kept staring down at the men, fidgeting, chattering as if she was trying to tell her something. *Hush, Pepper*, she told her. *They're going to notice movement in the window and look up. Stay still.*

But something had to be done. She thought she had better call Reggie. Maybe he could do something. He was the police after all. And he seemed to be a clever young man. She picked up the phone and stared at it. What was Reggie's number? Gosh, what was it? She tried and tried to remember, but her mind drew a blank. So she dialed 911 and waited, hoping that 911 would do the trick. Meantime, she watched Billy and Big Pete bring out another chest and wondered if this was something Josie knew about. Then, unexpectedly, the two men got in the pickup truck and promptly drove away.

Finally, after what seemed like an eternity, Reggie picked up the phone. She almost choked on her words as she explained.

"So now, Billy and Big Pete are driving away with the treasure."

"Are you sure?"

"No, I'm not. But what else could be in the chests? They were heavy. And in the middle of the night? There's only one thing they can be up to. They're stealing the gold. Well, some of it anyway. We've got to stop them."

"Oh, Margo, you keep pushing me to do things I'm not prepared for. How am I going to stop them? These are dangerous men, and I'm all alone."

"You have me. I'll come with you. We can't just let them get away."

"All right, then. Get dressed. I'll be there in five."

"That's too long. They're on the way."

"Well, they can't get through the tree clearing area. The machinery is still there, and the debris hasn't all been picked up yet."

"Then where are they going?"

"They could be heading for the wooden bridge over the creek. If the waters have receded enough, it could be passable already. I'll be right there."

Margo quickly got dressed and left her room, making sure that Pepper was safely locked inside. Then she tiptoed downstairs, hoping that Josie wouldn't hear.

When Reggie got to the hotel parking lot, Margo was already outside, pacing, crunching pebbles under her feet. The moon wasn't completely full anymore, but it was still bright enough to shed an illuminating silvery glow on everything. The night seemed so quiet, so peaceful. What a joke. Palmetto Bay was more like a den of pirates.

The air was cool in the early morning breeze and Margo shivered. The cicadas were chirping, telling the storm goodbye, and the lights from the moon and the parking lot reflected on the wet pavement creating oily rainbows in every puddle. She breathed in the fresh air, trying to wake up.

She saw the taillights of Reggie's patrol car approach and walked toward them hands in pockets, with a sense of finality. Her footsteps sucked up the mud that was sticking to her shoes, squeaking as she walked. Suddenly, she was sorry for Reggie, and for his car that was going to get muddy, and for all the misery and death she felt she had unwittingly caused the last few days. But above all, she was sorry for naïve Josie who had faith in that treacherous rat she called husband.

Margo was not deluding herself. Without a good plan in place, she was well aware of how inadequate this effort to stop the thieves was. How on earth could they stop them, just the two of them? Billy and Big Pete were violent, unpredictable, and ruthless, and very, very big. Reggie wasn't. And she was just a girl. But for Josie's sake, and for the sake of the people in the town, she couldn't just let them go. Not without making an effort at least.

Her eyelids were heavy with sleep. She felt a restless nervousness at being up at this early hour. Reggie looked exhausted too. And he didn't look very happy.

"To the bridge, then?" she asked when she hopped in the car, but all she got was a grunt. She crossed her hands on her lap and remained silent. She couldn't blame him for being upset.

Reggie drove carefully through the sleeping town. Driving through a sleeping town in the middle of the night is like driving through an otherworldly lucid dream. Streetlamps flickered their yellow lights, and the soft breeze shook and rustled the vegetation in the silvery penumbra. They passed a couple of cats in love at the mouth of an alley, and a starving stray dog further on, but nothing else. Margo put her window down a couple of inches so that the fresh air would help her stay awake. The night smelled of rotten vegetation and murder, and she wished she was far away.

"We've never had anything like this happen in Palmetto Bay before. I've never investigated a murder or chased a car down."

"I'm sorry, Reggie. It's probably my fault for digging up so many secrets."

"Nah, it's okay. At least old Grott didn't get away with murder again, and maybe Billy and Big Pete won't get away with the treasure."

"But maybe if Daisy hadn't come to get me, John and Jeanne would still be alive. And Gloria would be alive. I wish I had never gone up to the church."

"No point in blaming yourself, Margo. These things, they were already festering among us when you got here. We just didn't know it."

"I see two little red dots ahead. Headlights, you think?"

"We'll find out soon enough."

They drove on for a while in silence. Cool air poured into the front seat through the partially opened window, and Margo adjusted the jacket around her chest. The first dawn was already bathing the world in the magical early morning reds and yellows. They could see the road ahead a little better now, so Reggie stepped on the accelerator. They followed the road up the hill as if they had been going to Striker Grott's house, but they turned right at the intersection, where the road closely followed the hairpin twists and turns in the hills. It was a dangerous road, barely more than a dirt road, and Margo made sure to remain quiet.

"I've been thinking," Reggie said after a while.

"About how to capture them?"

"Yes. Actually, I thought that if we can get close enough to them to make out the model of the vehicle and the license plates, we can radio the State Police. Maybe they can intercept Billy and Big Pete when they get on the highway."

"That's a great idea. We don't stand a chance against them, just the two of us, especially if they're armed."

"I'm sure they are armed. They always are. So better hold on tight. This can get rough."

Reggie stepped on the accelerator, and the patrol car almost jumped forward. The sun was coming up from behind the hills. Enormous, swollen, it dazzled with its brightness every time the car turned in its direction, blinding Margo and the driver. Then the car would swerve at another hairpin turn, and the driver's face would fall into shadow. Reggie fumbled around for his sunglasses and breathed a sigh of relief when he found them.

"We're getting closer. I can almost read the license plate."

"Look, they're driving funny."

"I think they're drinking. Isn't that a bottle of something they're passing to each other?"

"I'm not surprised: the way they swerve from side to the side."

"Open the glove compartment. There should be a pair of binoculars in the bottom."

Margo rummaged in the glove compartment and found the binoculars. She also grabbed a pen and a strip of paper.

"Oh my God, what are they doing now?"

"They must have realized we're after them."

Margo stuck the binoculars to her eyes and stared at Billy driving recklessly from side to side. "I can see them clearly. Billy just yanked the bottle out of Big Pete's hands and he's drinking."

"Can you see the license plate?"

"Yes. Writing the number down."

"Okay, as soon as we clear this set of turns we'll have radio reception and I'll call it in."

Reggie was completely focused. He took the turns fast and steady. He was a good driver. He was in complete control. The rain of wet pebbles and splats of mud thrown up by the red pickup's tires blew onto their windshield wiper startling Margo every time, but Reggie didn't even flinch. At times he was almost blind from the flying debris, but he never lost control of the situation. He must have known the road like the back of his hand. Still as a dead mouse, Margo didn't dare say a word, not to distract him.

And then—just like that—they were clear of the hills. The horizon opened up in front of them as they began their descent. Half a mile ahead, the swerving truck had picked up the speed and was heading downhill completely out of control.

THE BLACK ROSE RETURNS

The valley was beautiful and wild. Where the Mississippi river—swollen by the violent rainstorms—flowed into Shark Bayou, the waters frothed and tumbled over each other, dumping the dirty looking, chocolate-colored liquid into the limpid blue sea.

All the vegetation was lush, fresh, and green. The sun shone on the moist leaves of the trees and the brush and made everything sparkle like a valley of diamonds. The sky was that absolutely, perfectly, clear blue, high pressure, not a cloud in sight. Flocks of birds flew above the valley in harmonious slowness, flapping their wings to unison, in loose formation.

Margo looked for the little bridge, the famous little bridge, but all she saw was the wild frothing of the river.

"I don't see the bridge, Reggie."

"Me either. It must have been washed away. It happens sometimes, during storm season. No. Look. It's there. It's just mostly covered by the water."

The red pickup had almost reached the bridge but was showing no signs of slowing down. Margo's heart started pounding hard. She grabbed tight to the door handle with one nervous, sweaty hand and held onto the binoculars in her lap with the other. She was horrified. Billy was driving straight into the rushing water. She didn't want to watch, but she was mesmerized at the same time and couldn't look away. She picked up the binoculars, and she blinked. Billy's face came into semi focus, and she thought she saw him grinning maniacally.

"They're not going to stop, are they?" she asked, knowing the answer in her heart.

"No, I don't think so. Billy might think they have a chance to cross. If the water wasn't so high, he would, but today, I don't know."

Reggie pulled over and stopped the car a couple of hundred feet from the river. They got out and stared. The air was chilly, and the froth from the roiling river shot up into the air and was carried by the wind toward where they stood. The wet droplets felt like tiny pinpricks on Margo's feverish skin. She wiped her face and neck with her hands. Overwhelmed, she couldn't stop shaking. As the seconds crawled forward in slow motion, she saw Reggie take out his cell phone and film the incident. After all, there was nothing he could do, and he had to file a report.

For a brief instant, the pickup slowed down. The chocolate brown waters were rushing forward with the speed of a freight train. She almost felt Billy hesitate. But it was a brief moment, for Billy revved up his engine and darted for the narrow wooden bridge.

It was sheer madness. It was a suicide mission. Maybe Billy felt the impossibility of his situation and decided it would be better to risk his life than be caught and thrown in jail. Maybe he truly felt he could make it. Point was that he went for it.

He gingerly maneuvered the pickup to the mouth of the bridge and wobbled onto the first wet wooden planks. He was a fearless driver. Even though the bridge was being tossed by the fury of the water from side to side, he hung on and kept on driving. He continued on steadily.

Margo couldn't believe her eyes. She was beginning to think that they would actually make it across and to safety. The pickup bravely made it to almost the halfway mark, and then, unexpectedly, it stopped. One of the wooden planks must have been washed away leaving a gap in the structure because the pickup was suddenly stuck, and it dipped as if one of the front tires had fallen into a hole. The waters rushed at it and covered the wheels and still it didn't move. It was going nowhere.

Horrified, her hand at her throat, Margo wondered what was going through Billy's mind. Impossible to open the doors and bail out, the way the water was pressing against them. It would have been useless anyway. Even if they managed to escape the truck, they would drown in the ferocious water. By now, they would be sitting waist-deep in water, and the pickup's engine would be dead. They might even be pinned down by their seatbelts—if they were wearing any.

The pickup shook and shivered under the onslaught of the powerful pounding water. It stood there clinging precariously to the little wooden bridge as Reggie and Margo watched horrified, unable to do a thing. Then, a taller, more powerful wave hit the side of the truck and it flipped sideways. It trembled on two wheels on its side like a circus act. But just for a couple of long and excruciating seconds. Then, without fanfare, it slipped into the froth and washed away. It floated for a short while, and they followed the rusty red color with their eyes as it swam away, mingling with the chocolate brown waters. And then it was gone.

"Josie is never going to forgive me." That was all Margo said and sat humbled and distraught all the way back to the hotel.

Time To Go

"I WISH YOU DIDN'T HAVE TO LEAVE YET. I feel like you barely did anything else but chase dead bodies. You could stay an extra day or two and enjoy the good weather. Recuperate, sort of."

Margo and Josie were drinking their steaming café au lait after a heartwarming breakfast of syrupy Couche-Couche.

"No, Josie, I can't. I better leave before I find another dead body." They both chuckled. "I better go. I was on my way to meet Pierre in Cypremort Point when I got stuck here, and if I don't show up again, he'll *make a bahbin*. But let's stay in touch. Let me know how things work out for you guys."

"I will. We're all very grateful to you. Before I forget, there was something I wanted to give you to show you my gratitude." Josie patted her hand gently and got up from the chair.

"You don't have to give me anything, Josie. I was glad to help."

"Wait here." Margo watched Josie go. No longer young, she was still a very pretty woman. She had the most gorgeous long, wavy hair when she let it loose, and she had an indefinable air of kindness and gentleness. She would find someone, for sure. Someone who would love her the way she deserved.

Meantime, Margo petted Pepper Paws, passing her hand over that soft, shiny, silky fur. Clever Pepper. Without her, she wouldn't have been able to solve all the mysteries of Palmetto Bay. Whoever said that cats had no special talents didn't know what they were talking about. *Take good care of your mom*, she told her.

Josie limped back slowly, favoring one of her legs. She hadn't asked, but judging from her bruises, the beating must have been brutal.

There was a small wooden chest in her hands. It was ornately carved and had jewels and pearls encrusted in the lid.

"This is the chest Billy wanted."

"Wow, it's beautiful, Josie. No wonder you didn't want to give it to him."

Josie laughed sadly. "Yes. I'm glad I had thought of hiding it because Billy looked for it really well. You saw the mess he left behind." She placed the chest on the table and opened it. It was lined in rotting green felt, now beginning to dry out. A few cracks had already appeared on the lid around the hinges, and the little box squeaked as it was opened. Soon, exposed to oxygen—out of the dead water environment that had preserved it—it would dehydrate and disintegrate, leaving nothing but a few remnants of the beauty it once was.

But as Josie opened the hinge, Margo squealed with delight when she saw that in it there was a tiny gold box, perfectly preserved. It was lucky that gold never rusted, and this Josie would be able to keep forever. It was shiny and intricately ornate with filigree designs, and inlaid with tiny precious stones. The whole thing was barely bigger than a bar of soap.

"When Billy was down there in the shipwreck, and they broke down the Captain's door, that's when they found the gold coins, stashed in one corner of the cabin. The other fishermen got so excited that they stopped looking for anything else. They had what they had come for. But Billy climbed over the debris to get to the other side of the cabin. He had seen a small object shine in the corner in a puddle of water, and it intrigued him. He quietly picked it up and slipped it into his backpack. He didn't tell the men about it. Then, when he got home, and we were alone in the bedroom, he took it out and showed it to me.

"These last few years, Billy's temper had been deteriorating. There were no jobs, there was no money, and he blamed me. He had moved to Palmetto Bay to be with me. Back then it had seemed like a promising future, and he was very much in love with me. But then the tourism declined, and money dried up. He had some rough years, but now, with the money, he felt that he could start over. He begged me to forgive him.

He promised to love me and cherish me the way he once had, and he swore he would never hurt me again. That's why he gave me these jewels."

Josie opened the tiny clip that held the filigree box closed, and its lid opened backward on unrusted hinges to reveal some small pieces of jewelry. There were half a dozen rings, and a few earrings, as well as other baubles, all tossed together in a jumble, as if in a hurry.

She moved the jewels aside with her index finger until she came upon a small ring. A sturdy, old fashioned gold ban held the intricate design of a rose no bigger than a thumbnail. In the middle of it, like a drop of dark red blood, sat a ruby, a perfectly untarnished ruby. Margo gasped and reached for it.

"This is the most beautiful ring I've ever seen in my life," she gushed.

Josie smiled, pleased at Margo's reaction. "I thought you'd like it. It's the prettiest ring in the box, and I think you should have it. Please don't say that you can't accept it. I would like you to have something to remember us by."

Margo's eyes teared up. It had been an emotional week, and she wasn't quite sure that she wanted to be reminded of it every time she wore the ring. But she smiled back at Josie and slipped the pretty ring on her finger.

"*Eh voila*, you see? It fits you perfectly. Now you really can't say no. That way you won't forget us. Margo looked up from her ring and saw that there was one lonely tear in Josie's eye.

"Thank you, Josie. I'll never forget you either."

Reggie showed up to say goodbye. Was that a hint of relief in his eyes? Most probably. It seemed to her that Reggie was the kind of small-town policeman who cherished an orderly and quiet rural life. He would enjoy checking on his people when they misbehaved, and answer a 911 call if someone needed help with a locked car door or a cat up a tree. But he had seen enough dead bodies to last a lifetime.

THE BLACK ROSE RETURNS

He and Josie brought her things out to the car and they hugged goodbye. Then it was time to give Pepper Paws back to her rightful mom. She kissed the cat's soft head with sadness. They had formed a strong bond, and she was going to miss her.

It was a wistful goodbye. They took a few pictures of each other—for Facebook, of course—and invitations were made and accepted, but they all knew they would never see each other again. Margo held back her tears and waved to them one last time as she drove past Josie and Reggie standing in front of the pub. With some luck she would be in Cypremort Point by lunchtime.

She stopped the car a mile out of town and got out where the centennial oak tree had fallen. It had been massive. No wonder it had taken so long to clear the road. The branches—cut down to manageable sizes—had been piled up on one side of the road, way back, out of the way. The leaves were already brown and shriveled. The wood itself had been chopped up and carted away. But the roots, sticking up toward the sky, had been left behind. Completely uprooted, they stood almost two stories high. It had been the only one to fall. Some of the smaller debris remained on the blacktop, but would soon wash away with the next storm.

What a quiet road. What a long and quiet road. There was no trace left of the vicious storm that had felled the tree. Bugs and birds chirped happily in the sun. Bushes rustled in the gentle breeze. With a sense of finality, she opened her car door and got back in. She was alone on the road except for a rusty, beat-up pickup truck approaching from the opposite direction. The driver—an old black guy with curly white hair—pulled his window down and signaled for her to stop.

Mark Driskoll And His Monkey

"MISS MARGO FONTAINE?" he inquired politely.

"Yes, that's me. How can I help you?" Please, not another dead body, she thought to herself with trepidation. She couldn't allow another murder to keep her in town.

"I'm Thomas Prejean, Miss. There's something I would like to show you before you leave." He sounded very insistent like he was not going to take no for an answer.

"I'm kind of in a hurry," she told him, hoping to be allowed to leave without having to be rude. After all, he was a stranger to her. Hadn't she been so critical of the castaway for having followed a stranger home?

"I understand. But I'm sure you would regret it if you missed it. It's about Mark Driskoll and his monkey. Please do follow me."

Intrigued, and against her better judgment, she followed the pickup. They headed back toward Palmetto Bay, and right before the first house, the pickup truck took a right turn onto an overgrown path and started climbing upward. A couple of twists and turns later, Margo found herself at the top of the cliff, overlooking the deep blue Shark Bayou.

"What are we doing here?" she asked Thomas Prejean when they got out of their cars. "That's the old church. And way back there, that's the bench where I found Gloria the policewoman dead."

"I know. That's why I brought you here. I have a story to tell you. Or rather, I have to tell you the end of a story. This is the old cemetery." They walked a gravel path that skirted the church in silence. The sun was beating down on Margo's head and she envied the old man's hat. They walked uphill a few more feet, and the path ended in front of the entrance to a decrepit cemetery, its old fashioned tombstones leaning away from the winds, crumbling. It was obviously no longer in use. Thomas Prejean unfastened the lock on the wrought iron gate and they entered. Maybe thirty tombstones stood in silence at diverse angles of falling, sticking their heads out of the overgrown shrubs. They had all been long forgotten. But at one side of the cemetery, one well-worn path had been kept clear. Here, at the end of the path, a handful of tombs overlooked the sparkling bayou, sunning themselves gently under the semi-shade of a sprawling oak tree. One tombstone in particular stood up straight as a ramrod. It had been covered in fresh flowers.

"This is the tomb of Mark Driskoll. Yesterday was the anniversary of his death." The old man approached the tomb and took his hat off.

"Mark Driskoll the explorer?"

"Yes. The same." Margo walked closer to the tombstone and bent down. She moved a wreath gently out of the way so she could read the inscription. "A quiet hero who shall never be forgotten. b.1855 – d.1935" she read. A smaller tombstone next to his was also well cared for. It simply read Maddock d.1935

"The monkey! These are the tombs of Mark Driskoll and Maddock the monkey. How is this possible?"

"That's why I asked you to come. I wanted to show you their tombs, and I wanted you to hear the end of their story."

"I read his diary, and I got the impression that he went down with the Camilla Star. But then I heard that he had managed somehow to survive. Everyone in Palmetto Bay seemed to have different versions of the story."

"He survived, Miss, and so did the monkey."

Thomas Prejean guided her to a stone bench overlooking the water and bid her to sit. Then he began his story.

"It was the year 1880. My grandfather, my Paw Paw, lived on a sugar plantation in Martinique, the island. Slavery had been abolished decades earlier and plantation owners had been ordered to let their slaves go, but the master hated to lose all that money so he sold them slaves to a merchant who was headed for Louisiana.

"As was the custom of the times, they were locked into the cargo hold of the ship and forgotten. But three days into the voyage, they were attacked by pirates. At first, when the cargo hold door was opened, my Paw Paw and the others thought that a miracle had occurred and they were being rescued, and they rejoiced, welcoming their saviors. They happily allowed themselves to be led to the other ship.

"Then, my Paw Paw looked up and saw the red Jolly Roger flag flying in the wind and realized what was going on. As they were lined up in formation on the deck of the new ship, they were made to watch how the crew and the passengers of their ship were massacred. They were terrified. They obediently marched down into the new ship's cargo hold, and they were locked in again. My Paw Paw heard the lock being driven into the door and felt a terrible sense of doom. But there was plenty of food and water, so they kept their hopes up and prayed, knowing that God wasn't going to abandon them to such a terrible fate and things would turn out for the best.

"But after a day or two, a terrible storm came up and soon the waves were beating the ship about without mercy. My Paw Paw and the other slaves threw up and got sick and started panicking about their fate. If the ship went down, they would all drown.

"They heard the main mast crack, and the ship listed. My Paw Paw and the other slaves never stopped praying. This was the opportunity to show their true faith. And they were rewarded when like a miracle—because what else could it be—they heard someone beating the lock on the trapdoor. He beat and beat at that door, and they sometimes heard him cry the word sorry over the fury of the storm. But he kept at it. Suddenly, my Paw Paw said, the trapdoor flew open and they were free. They scrambled up on deck and held onto ropes and nets so they wouldn't be blown over into the angry water, and realized that the lifesaver boats were still there, both of them. The sailors had been washed away, probably too drunk to think about lowering them. God had heard their prayers, and now they would be saved.

"They managed to pull them boats down and throw them in the water. Hard to believe as it was, they even managed to climb down the side of the listing ship and get in the boats. Despair lends us wings, Miss. That's what my Maw Maw used to tell us. Every single man, woman, and child got in them boats safely. A fire burning in a lighthouse on the far horizon told them that land was near, and so they sang hymns and prayed.

"It was almost impossible to row against the fury of the wind, but the waves were pushing them slowly toward the coastline. Every time they got close, they were pushed away again. But they kept on doing the only thing they could: row against the storm and try to stay in the boats.

And they kept their hopes up. On the second morning they opened their eyes, and the storm was over. They had fallen asleep on top of each other, exhausted after fighting the sea for two nights and a day. But they were all safe. And they saw that the land wasn't so far away.

"They rowed furiously, with renewed energy, and were startled by the screeching of a monkey. My Paw Paw, he almost fell out of the boat he got so startled when he saw that monkey. And by him, just a few feet to their left was a man—floating—tangled in debris. It was the flotsam that had kept him from drowning, you see. In his arms was the crying monkey that he was still holding like it was his baby.

"When they got close to the floating man, one of the women said, 'that's the man that opened the trapdoor. I saw him before he got washed off the deck.' Soon, others concurred. A number of them had seen the man go overboard with a big wave. But there was nothing any of them could have done, other than being thankful, but sorry for him.

"They rowed close to the flotsam, and they dragged the man and the monkey with them to shore. They landed on the beach, close to Palmetto Bay, by a cove, what they call the Pirate Cove these days, and they hid there."

"But why did they hide?"

"You must understand, Miss, that back then it was complicated to be a black man. They couldn't risk being discovered and taken to a plantation where they would continue to be worked and beaten to death. At least until they knew what the situation was, my Paw Paw and the others decided to remain hidden in the cove. There, they tended to the man for weeks until he was healed. There was a spring of fresh water in the cove. That was all they truly needed. Our ancestors had hunting and gathering skills, and these were remembered, so they didn't stay hungry for long. There were squirrels and raccoons, and plenty of alligators to roast. The monkey fended for itself, and once in a while even led them to where there were crops of fruits and vegetables.

"I guess that's the end of the story. Mark Driskoll healed and moved into the town. He was a white man, and very distinguished looking at that, so he had nothing to fear. Soon he was established and successful. And he never forgot his friends the slaves. At first, he brought them food and later helped them build homes and found a town of their own.

"So his descendants might still be living around here," Margo said.

"Indeed, Miss. If you've met anyone with very red hair and freckles, that'll be them. Freddy Mouton, the young man from the bait shop is one."

"Yup. I know Freddy Mouton and his mom. They both have red hair, very fair skin, and tons of freckles. And you say the monkey did all right as well?"

"It sure did, Miss. Mark Driskoll and his monkey, they died but a few days apart. They loved each other like kin."

"And who's been bringing them flowers?"

"We have. We're still grateful. We keep the graves clean, and every year on the anniversary of Mark Driskoll's death, we bring him and his monkey flowers. He'll never be forgotten. That's all I wanted to tell you. I'll be going now. You have a good day, Miss."

Thomas Prejean tipped a finger to his hat, and just like that, he was gone.

Thanks for reading! Please add a short review on Amazon, and let me know what you thought!

Don't miss the next Margo Fontaine Mystery:

The Golden Gift of Silence

Chapter 1

The Salt Dunes In August

THE SAND IS PRISTINE, WHITE, SOFT, CLINGY. The old man sits for a while under the beating, relentless sun. This far south, there's no shade anywhere. From where he's sitting, he can see the first ruins of what was once the original settlement, the one they call Old Town, and very, very far away, what appears to be a restaurant, nothing more than a run-down shack, jutting out into the bay. Everywhere else, the vast expanse of Louisiana's Shark Bayou.

The sun beats down on the old man's head mercilessly, not that he's complaining, even though his bald spot is burning away. He pats his pockets and feels the bulge the many bills make in them. Won't be long now. He tries not to think about what all he had to do to get his hands on all this money, and focuses on the shining waters of the bay. Any minute now, the boat will show up on the horizon, bobbing on the water with determination, bringing him a most certainly better future.

But time crawls at a miserable speed in the humid, empty expanse, and forces the old man to get up and pace. He can't keep still, thinking that he's been had. Anxiety mounts. His contact should have arrived already. He must have been duped.

The sun's too bright to look at the shimmering water, so he uses his hands as a visor against the glare and coughs up with relief, muttering something under his breath. That's him. He's coming, he tells himself. He's really coming. There, so far away that he can barely see it with his rheumy eyes, a tiny rowboat comes into view and soon gets bigger. Yes, it must be him, the old man thinks and starts hobbling toward the shore. There's a lot of money in his pockets, and it slows him down. The bundles loll from side to side as he tries to run on the dry sand and hit his thighs. What a sweet feeling, all that money on him. He grins a toothless grin and waves at the man rowing toward him.

The old man looks on anxiously. The newcomer throws down the oars and pulls in his boat onto the sand, and waves back in a cordial gesture as if they had always been friends. But they've only met once before. Briefly. The old man squints to take a better look at the younger man, but his eyesight is not what it once was. Still, he recognizes the voice and cries out.

"Good to see you. Did you get it?" he asks. He's not one to mince words. He can barely contain his impatience.

"You know I did. It was pretty easy, too."

"So let's see it," he says quickly, and a spray of saliva spurts out of his mouth. He steps toward the younger, leaner man. The greed and the excitement have turned his eyes shiny, almost translucent. He puts a shaking hand out. His arthritic fingers are slightly curved, like claws almost, and the younger man recoils, disgusted. The old man's sour breath comes out in jagged strips, hoarse, barely human, distorted by years of solitary confinement in a jail cell, and by lack of human contact.

He's almost forgotten how to talk to others, but the begging comes out clear. "I have to see it," he insists.

"Not so fast, old man. You have to show me the money first."

The older man knows that he should know better than to trust this stranger, but he has no choice in the matter. He looks at the young man's hungry smile and those long, sharp incisors that make him shiver with dread, and for a second he thinks about running away and forgetting all about this crazy adventure, but somehow, he feels that the matter is already out of his hands.

He sticks them into his pockets and pulls out the wads of money, all tied together neatly with blue fraying cord. He thinks about the years he's waited, the lifetime of suffering he still needs to redeem, and his hands shake. He shouldn't be here, he thinks. So much he could have done with this money. Why this obsession? Why?

"So how does it work?"

"I don't know," the old man says, shrugging. "I have to figure it out."

"Something tells me that you already know."

"No, no, I really don't. I've read about it somewhere, but they didn't know how to make it work either." The old man wipes the sweat off his brow and upper lip with the sleeve of his dirty, stained shirt. "Nobody does."

"If nobody knows, then you have no use for it, now do you?"

"What do you care if I have use for it or not? I paid for it fair and square."

"You paid me to steal it, but there was nothing fair or square about it." The young man laughs, sending a shiver down the old man's spine.

Before the old man can say anything else, the young man has already snatched the money out of his hands and is putting it away in his satchel.

When he sees that the young man is turning to walk away, he grabs him by the sleeve.

"Give it to me now, please. I've waited so long."

"You're naïve, old man. Did you really think I was going to give it to you? Then, you're a fool." And with that, he turns around and starts walking toward the shore, where he has left his rowboat sitting on the sand.

With a yelp of despair, the old man follows—as fast as he can—despair giving him the speed and the strength to keep up. He's sobbing softly now. "You have to let me see it," he says, catching up, and grabbing the man's arm. "At least let me see it," he begs. But the young man refuses to stop, refuses to acknowledge him.

Angry now, with the last bit of strength he has left, the old man grabs at the satchel and pulls. Surprised at his own strength, he pulls harder now and yanks the satchel off the younger man's shoulder. He's learned a move or two in his long, twisted life, and is pleased that he can still stand his ground if he has to. He clutches the unseen object to his chest possessively, unwilling to let it go. Over his dead body, he tells himself.

But the young man reacts with fury. His face gets red, and his eyes narrow. He lunges at the old man. This sudden violence terrifies the old man. He steps back, hanging on to his heart's desire, and turns to run, as if he, himself believed that he would be able to. But it's pointless.

In the blink of an eye, he's rolling on the sand with the younger man, in a fight to the death. He refuses to let the satchel go. The more the other man pulls and punches, the harder he hangs on. There's sand in his eyes, and his nose, and in between his few remaining teeth. Again and again he questions his own sanity, but he will not let go.

All of a sudden, a strong, cold, burning, searing hot pain rushes into his chest, and he forgets to breathe. It takes him a few seconds to grasp that he's been stabbed. He grabs on to his belly—where the pain is worst—and tries to catch his breath.

As he turns on his back and looks up at the punishing blue sky, a feeling of confusion fills his soul, and he comprehends that something's wrong. He's getting colder, losing contact with his hands and feet. He's bleeding out. He touches his side where the pain is most excruciating and feels the hot sticky mess oozing out from between his fingers. He realizes, surprised, that he's dying.

At least the pain is subsiding now, but the world is fading around him. It's losing importance. He wonders if there's still time to believe in God and beg for forgiveness, you know, just in case, and thinks about how he's done too much evil in this life to be forgiven.

Then he remembers his mother. How odd. He hasn't thought about her in years. She was a kind woman, gone too young. At least she didn't live long enough to see him become this unloved, homeless mess. Then he has a glimmer of hope that maybe she'll be there on the other side, waiting for him. And finally, with tears of sadness and regret, he closes his eyes and prays, you know, just in case.

Chapter 2

The Murderer

THERE WAS THE OLD MAN, pacing on the shore. God only knew how long he had been waiting for him. Poor guy. He turned the artifact in his hands and pondered.

Since the beginning of this whole thing, he had been shocked by his own behavior. He had never stolen anything in his life and never expected to be so exhilarated by it. But driven by an inexplicable impulse, he had slipped into a friend's library and stolen. He remembered touching the artifact for the first first time, and the strange and wild thrill that rushed through his blood when he smoothly slipped it into his satchel. Not a pang of regret, shame on him. It was the most exciting thing he had done his whole life. He smiled wickedly to himself. He didn't expect anyone to ever suspect a respectable person like himself of the theft.

And then, as he turned around to slip out as quietly as he had entered, he saw the collection of knives there—right in front of him—in a glass-topped table cabinet full of antique wonders. He tried the latch and almost laughed out loud when he found it unlocked. Before he had a chance to rationalize what he was doing, he picked up a broad blade knife—a machette—sharp, etched with exotic markings that looked like Japanese man'yōgana, beautifully kept, and he turned it this way and that, admiring it. Then, he slipped it carefully into his satchel next to the artifact and hurried back to the door. He closed the door behind him, smoothed his hair with his left hand, and straightened his tie, and then he hurried back to the party to mingle with the other guests before he was missed.

Staring at the slowly approaching shore, he watched the bent figure pacing back and forth, and he felt sorry for the old man. He thought about turning back, knowing deep inside that he would do no such thing. So he kept on rowing. It was hard work that he wasn't used to, the rowing. His shoulder blades and his arms were on fire.

At what point did he decide to keep the artifact? Hard to say. It just happened. A small school of colorful fish swam by his boat, and one of them lagged behind and looked up at him. It was at that moment he knew. Whatever it took, he was keeping the artifact. Whatever it took. And that was final.

But once he began rowing away from the beach and the murder, the enormity of what he had just done rocked his soul, and he began to shake. Did he deplore the killing of a harmless old man? Well, of course he did, on some deeper level. He was no killer. But it was too late for regrets. He should have turned the boat around from the beginning, but he didn't. Instead, he talked himself into going ashore to explain himself, to let the old man know that he had changed his mind. Can't let him stand in the sun all day without an explanation, right?

And the whole thing had turned into a disaster. The old man had grabbed his satchel and refused to let go, so this horrible anger welled up in him, coming out of nowhere, and before he could figure out how to control himself, a hand—his own hand—had grabbed the Japanese machette he carried by his side, and buried it in the old man's chest. Still angry, he yanked the satchel from the dying man's hands, and by the sound of tinkering inside it, knew it was broken. It wasn't until that moment that he realized that in the scuffle for the knife, he had been slashed too.

He howled in anger and could have killed the old man again. He stomped away toward his boat trying to control his breathing and his fury. The old fool had not only wounded him but broken his precious artifact, and now what was he going to do? For now, he had to get away before he was seen. He looked around before jumping in the boat but saw that there was nothing to be worried about. He was all alone on this side of the universe. He looked down at his chest and the ever-expanding bloodstain on his shirt. It would be okay, he decided. It didn't hurt too much.

He rowed for a while before heading for the rocky bend that signaled the beginning of Old Town and stopped. The stolen machette lay where he had left it, in the bottom of the boat. He should toss it overboard, out here, so far from shore that nobody would even think to look for it. But he picked it up and held the beautifully etched piece, and something in him kept him from throwing it away. It was a beauty, and he was a lover of beautiful things. Maybe he could find a place to hide it until the unfortunate death got forgotten. It's worth the risk, he told himself. I'll store it, hide it, and then when it's safe, maybe sell it, maybe not. But I will never throw it away.

He grabbed the machette by the hilt and dipped it carefully in the water. For a second, the water ebbed around the blade, and it became tinted with the fresh blood. But there was so little of it really, that within seconds the red tinge got diluted, and it was gone. Then, remembering that there was blood all over his shirt, he took that off carefully because already the fabric was beginning to stick to the wound and rinsed it out in the water as well. Good thing it was a dark shirt. Good thing that it was a sunny day, and it would dry soon. As to the pain, well, it wasn't unbearable.

He stared at the shore for a while. He was so far now that he couldn't see the body any longer. The gentle waves lapped against the rowboat as he sat there, contemplating the enormity of what had just happened. But there was no point in sitting there. What was done couldn't be undone. So, he picked up the oars, and he rowed again. He navigated around the salt cliffs of the bend, careful not to hit the rocks that jutted out treacherously from under the water, careful not to make any sudden moves that would make the pain worse, and then he headed for home.

About the Author

Agnes Makóczy is a freelance writer and adventure traveler. Always on the road, she finds inspiration for her stories in the places she travels to. She's the author of the *Margo Fontaine Mysteries*, a series that takes place in the fictional seaside town of Half Moon Bay, in South Louisiana, the land of swamps, alligators, haunted hotels and plantation homes, where well-kept secrets, and the stories of old Southern families, will conspire to keep you reading into the night.

Ms. Makóczy loves to write. After brief attempts at Romance Novels and one Health book, she's had to face the truth: she loves writing Murder Mysteries the best.

To read about her other books and upcoming works, please visit:

www.agnes-makoczy.com